The Elixir

A Bud Hutchins Urban Fantasy

JB MICHAELS

To Ashley, the love of my life, without you this book would never have been written. Thank you, my love.
To Molly and Emily, thanks for always being so supportive.
To Jenna, honorary member of the Order, whose enthusiasm keeps me writing.

PRAISE FOR THE WORKS OF JB MICHAELS

"Michaels is beyond imaginative; he takes the reader into a realm of marvel and wonder. The story is spunky, witty, humorous and filled with endless action. There is a never a dull moment."

-- Readers' Favorite

"A lively tale whose highly skilled, pint-sized heroes provide endless fun."

-- Kirkus Reviews

"...kept smiling throughout this exciting, original and very entertaining book."

-- Readers' Favorite

"The book is packed with a sense of adventure and exuberance and leaves you wanting more when it is finished."

-- Readfulthings Blog

"From the opening pages to the final sentence, you're treated to a rollercoaster ride of fun and frights."

-- Amazon Reviewer

Visit MisterMichaels.com, the official site of Author JB Michaels for TWO FREE BOOKS!

The Works of JB

With over 500 pages of action adventure and thrills, these individual books have earned a recommended Kirkus review, 3 awards, 11 five star badges from Readers' Favorite and over 50 positive reviews on Amazon.

The Order of St. Michael: A Bud Hutchins Thriller

The Tannenbaum Tailors and the Secret Snowball *(Gold Medal- Readers' Favorite International Book Awards 2017) (National Indie Excellence Award Finalist)*

The Tannenbaum Tailors and the Brethren of the Saints *(Kirkus Reviews Recommended Book) (Bronze Medal-Readers' Favorite International Book Awards 2017)*

TABLE OF CONTENTS

1	Concentrated Rage	1
2	Bud P.i.	3
3	Parental Obstruction Obstructed	9
4	Showing Off	13
5	Unleashed	16
6	Disinterred	20
7	Capone	23
8	Ivy Out Of Her League	27
9	Covington Calling	30
10	Floating Investigation	34
11	Windowing	38
12	Concentrated Ebb And Flow	41
13	Bud Meets Ivy	43
14	No Exit	46
15	Illusory Institution	49
16	Ghoulish Gallery	53
17	Mummified Remains	58
18	Lab Of Renown	63
19	Blockade And Beeper	66
20	Blockade Run	70
21	Maeve And Mary Sitting In A Tree...	74
22	...K-I-L-L-I-N-G	77
23	Ghostly Guardians	80
24	Sears Tower Of Terror	84
25	Bedknobs No Broomsticks	90

26	Sinkholes And Surprises	94
27	Rampage	98
28	Lion Head	102
29	Medieval Time	106
30	Violated	109
31	Hubris	111
32	Unconventional	116
33	The Proper Application	120
34	Historical Implications	124
35	The Mummy	127
36	Deus Ex Martinez	131
37	Elixir Of The Ancients	134
38	Monsters Of The Midway	139
39	Hyde In Hyde Park	143
40	Save Maeve	148
41	Save Ivy	152
42	Canary In A Coal Mine	156
43	The Order Power	159
44	Resolute And Irresolute	162

1

CONCENTRATED RAGE

The glass beakers shattered, victims of the man's frustration. So close, but the elixir still needed more work. Probably different ingredients. He would have to start from square one. The year of research had failed him. He rested on the chair next to the long table of glass tubing, microscopes, petri dishes. He wanted to destroy the rest of his workspace, but that would set him back further. There was something missing, even the world's libraries bore nothing new for his research. He had considered a sabbatical many times, but the time was past for that. The board's decision would be final within weeks.

He stood up and looked at broken glass on the floor. He sighed and grabbed the broom that hung on the wall. The single light bulb cast just enough light to catch the glass shards strewn across the floor. He methodically swept in a controlled manner that belied his earlier rage. His outbursts were becoming more and more frequent. Many people had told him to perhaps seek anger management. He had no time for it. Too much to do.

He wanted to avoid going to the Institute. His relationship with the Institute was strained after the last incident, yet he knew that the contents of the Institute would be the only way forward. He finished shuffling the broken bits of glass into the dustpan, emptied it into a small blue recycling bin, and pulled the string of the singular light bulb. There was no way to see in the room when the light was off. No ambient light from the outside. He secured his phone and lit the flashlight, then walked over to a grey steel door. He pulled down a large handle that released the hatch. Still no light.

2

BUD P.I.

"Bert. I think it dreadfully silly, downright superfluous, that I am in this position." Bud lay on branch in a tree high above a residential street in the Lakeview neighborhood of Chicago.

"Sir, if you want this new technique to work than you must help activate it," Bert responded through Bud's earbud.

"Why do we always develop remote activation last? We should make it a priority before we even test any other aspect of any new contraption. For the love of all that's heavenly," Bud said, exasperated at how high he was from the street.

Bud pushed a mirrored button on the drone that he and Bert were field testing. The drone's quad-copter propellers spun, pushing away the smaller leaves attached to fig-like branches. It hovered in place. Bud gripped his mobile phone tight while still prone on the branch. He searched for the right app.

"Bert, I thought you said you would finish the app icon. I hope this is the bloody right one!"

"Sir, I think you should prep the piloting controls on your mobile. The couple is arriving," Bert said.

"Great. Just wonderful. Ready the remote teleportation program if I fall from this blooming tree as I will not be able to initiate it whilst fearing for my life."

A black Audi rolled up the residential street. Bud could see two people in the front cabin of the car. No hands on the wheel. The car's self-drive program had been initiated.

"Bert you may be obsolete. This Audi is driving independent of external manipulation," Bud said.

"I really believe you should learn how to drive Bud. Reliance on technology was almost your undoing with Brother Mike," Bert fired back.

"You saved me. So your point is quite ironic my android friend."

The Audi parked in front of a large new two-flat, red brick apartment building. A blue 'W' flag waived from the porch. The Cubs fans of the vehicle disembarked. One was a young blond woman with glasses and a short, shapely figure. The other person was an older man with a pipe jutting from his mouth and patches on the elbows of his tweed jacket.

Bert's robotic voice startled Bud. "That should be Dr. Covington."

"Yes, and as Mrs. Covington suggested, the other person is a teacher's assistant at Chicago Met University, Tricia Pazinski. I am starting the drone's camera operation now Bert."

"You should have done so already Bud."

"I am trying not to fall from this giant tree Bert to my inevitable death."

"I would have started the camera when informed the car was on approach. Just saying."

"Again, remote activation would have been welcome. Now shut it. I am attempting to concentrate." Bud piloted the drone off the branch and it hovered high above the couple, who opened the gate to a porch walkway. The drone's quad-copter design worked to limit the noise. Two propellers alternate operation so that all four do not fire at the same time. Bud moved the drone a good 25 feet above the couple.

"We need more evidence to convince Mrs. Covington of her husband's infidelity Bert. I am going to have to make the drone follow them in."

"I agree with you sir. There are no windows, curtains, or blinds open. Initiate the cloaking tech when you see fit. It drains too much battery and does not last long."

"I know that Bert. We designed it together. Are you getting the recording?"

Bud moved the drone high above the front door and waited while Tricia, the teacher's assistant held the storm door open, and Covington turned the key in the lock.

Bud looked at his mobile phone's screen. He touched the settings icon and the screen showed invisibility was an option. He pushed it. A warning popped up on the screen: 'This feature will significantly drain the drone's battery. Dismiss. Never Show again.' Bud shook his head and dismissed the alert.

The drone disappeared. To anyone who didn't know what to look for it was invisible. To those who did, a distortion of light, similar to the effect of a floating mirror, gave it away.

"I am receiving the drone's feed Bud. You are good to go. You might want to hurry."

The couple moved to enter the two-flat. The storm door was closing. Bud fumbled the phone and the drone flew up instead of down. With one hand he saved the phone from its crash on the gravel below, only his other hand and leg still gripped the branch. He pulled himself up and flew the drone down to the doorway, but the storm door closed. Bud failed.

"Shit. Shit. Shitty shits." Bud swore profusely.

"Not good sir, perhaps we can wait 'til they come back out."

The storm door opened again. Tricia Pazinski had left her book bag on the porch.

"Oh yes yes!" Bud yelled from the tree. She stopped and looked up towards the tree. The teacher's assistant shook her head then looked away.

Bud piloted the drone into the house. Then shut his mouth.

"Sir, you don't have much battery left with the cloak initiated."

The low battery icon blinked in the drone app. Bud needed to rely on the app and the camera feed to pilot the drone. The drone itself hugged the ceiling in the front hall of the Covington's home. Mr. Covington entered the doorway and grabbed Tricia and pulled her for a passionate kiss. She pulled away to stop her bag from getting caught in the storm door. Covington grabbed her bag and threw it in the house. He pulled her close and resumed kissing her. She kissed him back this time. Coats hit the floor. The drone's camera, positioned on the bottom of the drone, caught the footage with a bird's eye view. The drone began to drop. Bud saw the battery was only 10 percent.

"Bert you are getting this?"

"Yes sir. We should have enough evidence to convince Mrs. Covington of her husband's foul behavior. How on earth will you get the drone out of the house Bud?"

The couple had left the front hall and were well away from the drone. The drone's microphone did pick up faint moaning from somewhere in the interior.

"Let's hope they left the door open with their passionate ignorance Bert."

Bud pushed the button of his teleportation wristband. He was out of the tree and now on the street next to the Audi. Bud hurried to the front door. He turned off the invisibility feature of the drone; the battery was down to five percent. A crash would certainly alarm the couple no matter how intense their love-making session.

Bud reached the storm door. It was open. He reached for front door. Open. The drone fell from the ceiling. Bud reached out with his gangly arms and caught the drone.

"Time to go."

Bud hit his wristband and disappeared.

3

PARENTAL OBSTRUCTION OBSTRUCTED

Bud walked past a "For Sale" sign post on the front lawn of an old ranch home with brown brick. It was different than his smaller home he grew up in. He had taken up residence in his grandfather's vacant home. The house smelled like smoke from years of his grandmother smoking. She had passed away ten years prior. Lung cancer. Bud was merely ten years old, yet he had fond memories of her. She'd been a very strong-willed opinionated woman who would have made a great columnist. Bud often thought she could have even won a Pulitzer Prize had she pursued a career in journalism, yet the generation she grew up was not accepting of working women.

His grandfather went missing about a year ago, but Bud believed him to be alive. Bud had spent most of the previous year teleporting to places his grandfather had already been according to the photos around the house. Bert had set up shop in the back office. His entire computer console and charging station sat near the cat 5 cable box that connected to the internet and into any database Bud and Bert needed to hack.

The furniture had not been moved for years. The walls were stained from the smoke and carpet was original to the house. Bud relived his fondest memories of his childhood in this home every time he entered. His parents wanted to sell it. Bud refused to move out. He walked to Bert's office.

"Bud! Glad you made it back with the drone intact! I shall charge it for you. Your parents have arranged a showing of the house this evening at 7pm. There will be a full moon tonight. We should be able to scare them off fairly easily."

"Oh jolly good, Bert. Jolly good." Bud handed Bert the drone then headed to the kitchen for a bottle of water. A note was on the fridge. "Bud, this is your mother. There is a showing tonight. Please leave the house. Mom."

He shook his head. Her redundancy was insulting. Why she insisted on telling him it was her twice? Made no sense. There was no postscript that said love you. Bud's relationship with his parents was strained, indeed.

Bud sighed and threw the note into the garbage. He grabbed some leftover Chinese food and spread it over the floor. He chuckled. That might even deter someone from buying the home before they even got to the basement.

Bud walked down the steps. In one corner was the washer and dryer and a pile of clothes, and in the other there was a door with an open padlock. Bud removed it and walked in. It was quite cold in the room. The entire room was a freezer. He found her sitting on the floor of the freezer room. Bud, for years, refused to wear anything save his trench-coat but since the Beauregard zombies destroyed it, he now wore a leather jacket in an attempt to look like a tough mobster.

"How are you feeling today Maeve?"

"Okay. Looking forward to tonight. It is a full moon isn't it?" Maeve's voice was similar to Bert's. It was the best they could do with the artificial voice box they implanted to replace Maeve's undead throat that was ripped away by a monk-turned-werewolf of the Order of St. Michael, a sect of the Catholic Church stationed at trees around the world to stave off evil spirits.

"Yes, I shall lock you up as usual. Any more decay or has the freezer done well to slow it?"

"I think I look pretty good given the circumstances." She pointed to the mirror in the freezer. Her hazel eyes and face were in a perpetual scowl. The nerves in her face were fried. When she talked, the sound came from her throat. Maeve, a gifted monk of the Order of St. Michael, was made undead by zombie Confederate veterans at the Beauregard plantation a few months ago. Her ability to absorb supernatural abilities had saved her life...in a way.

"Any progress on achieving my reanimation?" Maeve asked.

"We just closed another adultery case so we should be able to fund more of the equipment needed to help sustain your heartbeat after you transform," Bud said.

"Oh good. I don't know how much longer I can sit in this freezer. This is no way to not live, hahaha." Maeve's voice was robotic and could not really convey any inflection.

Bud smiled at her. "Well, it is nearly time. Remember you can be as noisy as you like."

Bud walked out of the room. He placed the padlock back on the bracket, but forgot to lock it.

4

SHOWING OFF

Bud and Bert watched a young couple walk up to the front door of Bud's grandfather's home. The possible buyers were greeted by an older woman who wore fancy, flashy clothes; a silver blouse, long dangly earrings and lots of makeup-- which Bud knew matched the veteran realtor's personality. She smiled and shook the couple's hands with a flourish. Her charismatic salesperson skills would be no match for Maeve.

"Do you think it wise that we sit here in the car?" Bert stared at the party about to enter the home.

"It matters not what I think. We have to do this for the sake of my Grandfather. He needs his home when we find him. Also, it makes for a good bit of fun to watch them scurry out of the house like fools." Bud leaned forward in the passenger seat of their red beater car.

The showing began. The interested couple and realtor entered the home. The kitchen would be a mess of Chinese leftovers and in the basement they would be met by Maeve's guttural growls.

Bud looked up at the full moon.

Maeve convulsed and tore down the shelf that Bert fastened to freezer wall for her just a day ago. Her undead heart began to beat. Her hair follicles suddenly came alive, and she grew more hair on her head. A silver streak flowed like a river from scalp to stomach. Her nerves began to fire with pain. Comfortable pain. The pain of being alive satiated Maeve during her transformation, but soon that pleasure would give way to her hunger. In the freezer lay meat that Bud bought for her transformations. She bounded over to a new package of steak and tore it open. Maeve ate like the feral beast she was. She bit into the meat with sharp, drooling canines. A light in the basement turned on. She could see it through a crack between the door and the jamb.

She threw down the meat and bounded toward the open door. She smashed through it on all fours. Her hair covered her face. A silver streaked monster rushed towards the realtor.

"'Aaaaaaah! What in god's name?!'" The realtor fell to the floor. Her cellphone flew through the air. The couple who had been behind her on the house tour ran up the stairs.

Maeve pinned the realtor to the floor and smelled the realtor's neck. Her perfume pleased Maeve's rejuvenated sense of smell. The werewolf opened her mouth wide and with her newly restored vocal chords, growled in the realtor's face.

Bud and Bert saw the couple emerge from the house screaming and flailing their arms. The man fumbled for his keys. The woman grabbed them from him and unlocked the door to their white SUV. They sped off down the dimly lit residential street.

"I take it our resident she-wolf succeeded in quelling our real estate issues for now," Bud said, smiling.

"On the contrary sir, three people entered the house. Only two exited." Bert gave Bud a blank stare.

"The realtor. Oh shit." Bud opened the passenger door and ran to the house.

5

UNLEASHED

A growling, feral Maeve burst through the front door just as Bud reached the walkway. The storm door's hinges bent from the force of a beast unleashed. The door was now broken and partially off the frame. Bud stopped and put his hands forward as if to tame Maeve. The long white streak of her hair was the most visible to Bud until she stood up and showed her hairy face. Pearly white canines dripped with drool, not blood, Bud noted.

"Maeve, my dear, it is effusively imperative that you cease, desist, and mar--, well, bound back down to the basement. You are a danger to your fellow man and you are a sworn monk of the Order of St. Michael."

Maeve cocked her head and howled. Her foul breath blew Bud's hair back. He pinched his nose. His ears ached.

Bert approached from behind Bud. Maeve bolted away from them and headed south down Fairfield Avenue.

"Bert, you dolt. You scared her off."

"I seriously doubt I scared her Bud. She probably knew I could help you stop her."

"That is exactly what you will do. Let's get in the car and give chase. We must save her from murdering some unfortunate person or persons." Bud and Bert ran to their red Pontiac.

"What about the realtor, sir?"

The fancily dressed realtor fixed her hair as she emerged from the home fumbling for her keys. She checked around to see if the coast was clear.

"There she is now." Bud pointed then yelled to the re-altor, "Not to worry, the beast is quite clear of this locale!"

"Let's hope the vehicle can match Maeve's speed," Bert said. He entered the car in his stiff, robotic fashion.

"She is heading south. Whatever for...I wonder." Bud sat in the passenger seat. He preferred to sit in the back, but this instance required a wider field-of-view. The car rumbled to a start.

Maeve tore down the street towards 87th street on the southside of Chicago. Bud tracked her location from his mobile device. She showed up as an orange blip on his map application. She moved steadily and with impressive, sustained speed.

"We can cut her off if we head, with great haste, down California Avenue then make a left."

"Sir, my protocols only allow me to go 5 mph over the speed limit," Bert, Bud's android assistant stated.

"Bert...Damnit. I programmed you that way for safety reasons. Undo your damn programming at this critical juncture."

"You have yet to implant me with voice commands to implement modifications to my vehicular protocol." Bert drove down California avenue at about 25 mph.

Bud slapped his forehead. He looked at Maeve's location. She was moving at a faster pace than Bert could drive the car, she was getting faster. Her speed was up to 35 mph. Her comfort with her newfound agility was progressing quickly. This was the first time she was able to stretch her legs in wolf form. She was supposed to be in the basement. Bud remembered that he may have left the room unlocked.

Maeve burned past 87th Street on her way to 95th Street. Bud and Bert were stopped at the light on 87th.

"Maeve is moving with purpose. But to where? Bert, what is south of here that would be of interest Maeve?"

"Sir, the southern tip of Chicago is known for its burial grounds. There is a monk of the Order of St. Michael stationed at Mt. Olivet cemetery on 111th Street and California Avenue, near Alternate Reality, the best comics shop in town."

"You mention the comics shop now! I need to update you. Let's keep heading south. If she stops before the cemetery, then I will press your right foot with my left foot to increase pressure on the accelerator. Her only reason to stop would be most likely to puncture someone's jugular vein. There are only residential neighborhoods and Catholic elementary schools between here and there." Bud furrowed his brow and looked at Maeve's location, willing her to keep moving.

Bert followed protocol and pursued her at the speed of 30 mph as they approached 95th Street. Maeve neared 107th Street, a few blocks from Mt. Olivet.

6

DISINTERRED

The full moon loomed large in the sky above Mt. Olivet Cemetery. Maeve stretched her back and arms as she stood up. Her long black hair with white streak fell over her back and partially spilled over the front of her shoulders. Her black hoodie and jeans were intact, mostly. There were tears at the extremities by her large clawed hands and feet. Her skin was covered with dark brown fur. Her jaw jutted slightly, caused by the growth of her canines. Her heart beat fast. Maeve breathed deeply. The chill air was a comfort. Any feeling she experienced was a comfort. In wolf form, she was alive again. When she had emerged from Bud's Grandfather's home, she had followed a strong scent. She smelled it every time she was locked in the basement and in wolf form. She finally was able to follow it tonight. The smell was coming from this cemetery.

She entered the cemetery with a single leap. The moonlight showed old gravestones, mostly dating from the 19th century. They were large and expensive--marble and stone with symbols adorning the tops. There were gothic mausoleums perched at the top of the hill. Down the hill were rows and rows of graves. Maeve moved to the interior of the cemetery. Trees lined the paths. One of the trees was, assuredly, a gateway that a monk of the Order was assigned to protect. Perhaps that was the source of the smell.

Maeve moved further into the cemetery and ascended the hilltop towards the mausoleums at the crest. There were trees up there. The scent grew stronger. She reached the top of the hill and down the path saw a police squad car. Parked. No lights were on. Maeve quickly dropped on all fours, bounded off the path and used the tombstones for cover as she approached. The squad car's passenger door and rear passenger side door were open. Maeve stood back up and examined the car closely. There was an unconscious police officer inside, leaning on the passenger door. Another officer's head rested on the steering wheel. Maeve noticed their sidearms were missing. Normal chatter and codes burst forth from the radio. The rack that usually held a bigger weapon was bent and broken. The shotgun missing.

The source of the odor had to have been here. It was strongest in this area.

A piercing, booming, sound resonated in the cemetery and rattled Maeve's sensitive ear drums. A bullet smacked up against the front passenger door, which Maeve stood behind. Another shot hit the window. It cracked. Maeve ducked behind the cover of the door. She waited to see if another shot would ring out. Nothing. She surmised that the gunman was near the mausoleum closer to the entrance. She bounded back to the tombstones for cover. Then she saw him--a man dressed in a cream trench coat and a suit that matched the jacket. He wore a fedora cocked to the left. The man's face bore a large scar. Al Capone had risen from the dead. ***The notorious world-famous gangster and king of Prohibition lived again.***

7

CAPONE

Bud and Bert stopped at the gate of Mt. Olivet Cemetery. They heard a gunshot. Bud emerged from the car quickly. He bonked his head on the door frame.

"It is most upsetting that we hear a shot at where Maeve stopped." Bud rubbed his head. He threw a destination marker over the gate and initiated teleportation. Without the marker in an open area, Bud could teleport into a gravestone mixing his molecules with the stone, thus death would ensue.

He vanished from outside the gate and appeared on the other side.

"Sir, couldn't you have just climbed the gate?" Bert said. His head hung out the driver window.

"Bert, another lecture from you and I may have to shut you down completely. Stay in the bloody car."

Bud shuffled towards Maeve's signal. He looked at his phone and saw that she had stopped in the center of the cemetery near the top of the hill. Another shot rang out. Bud moved faster. His goal was to find Maeve and have them both teleport back home.

Maeve moved closer to Capone. Her hand and footfalls were silent with her padded feet. Capone scanned the area, she could see his short, stout silhouette in the moonlight, guns held waist-high. He scanned the area. Maeve noticed a bluish glow emanating from him. The moonlight was not capable of this illumination. He was corporeal, which meant he was able to inflict physical damage. He grimaced in frustration at not finding his prey, but kept to the path and walked towards the squad car.

Maeve hid behind a Celtic cross tombstone, right alongside him. She leapt out from her hiding spot and attacked his arms. Capone reeled and fell to the ground, dropping the guns but somehow his fedora stayed on his head. Maeve slashed at his face. The scar opened. His blood was blue. Capone pushed Maeve away and stood up. He stuck his chin out and bit his bottom lip. He grabbed her by the hoodie and landed two hard hitting bombs with his ring laden-right fist. Maeve growled and bit his left arm. Capone's brow furrowed and he threw her off his arm with incredible strength. She flew into the front grill of the squad car. Maeve's back felt like it was on fire. The pain blanketed her entire body. She almost wished to be in zombie form again.

Capone examined the bite wound. Then from his trench coat, he pulled the police shot gun. He pumped it and prepared to deal more damage to Maeve.

Bud heard the fighting, the howling, the pained verbal exclamations. He reached the top of the cemetery's one rolling hill. He didn't have time to process what he saw. Al Capone was alive and well. Bud was sure that his body had been moved from Mt. Olivet Cemetery to a place on the north side of town.

"Was that merely a ruse to divert people away from his actual grave that is still safely hidden here at Mt. Olivet?" Bud spoke out loud, but his words were interrupted by his heavy breathing. He wasn't used to running. He saw Maeve crouched near the front of a squad car. He saw Capone moving closer to her, prepping a death blow. Maeve jumped towards Capone and pinned him to the gravel. She unleashed a flurry of claws. A ferocious mauling.

Bud thought, "Perhaps I should intervene." Seeing her so violent bothered him.

"Maeve! Maeve! I cannot believe I am running towards a werewolf and a notorious gangster! I think you have handled the situation quite thoroughly!" Bud ran to the opponents.

The ghostly Capone was a blue bloody mess. His face was literally covered with scars. Maeve shoulders and chest raised and lowered quickly. She stepped back from the mess of Al Capone. She looked up at Bud then fell to the ground in a growl.

Bud ran to Maeve, who, in wolf form, was badly injured. The need to repair her to a healthy state was ever more pressing. When the moon went down she would go back to being undead. If she wasn't repaired, this would further damage whatever tissue was worthy of saving.

He held her and watched Capone's form vanish. All that was left were bones. Whatever supernatural menace resurrected the bones of the gangster was still at large.

8

IVY OUT OF HER LEAGUE

Ivy Zheng walked through the broad, heavy, medieval wooden double doors of the Archaeology Institute at Chicago Metro University. The lobby had a small gift shop to the right of the entrance and an info desk on the far wall that usually had a volunteer monitoring bags that needed checking for those interested in walking the gallery of the Institute. It was after hours so no one was at the desk. Ivy walked to the left away from the gallery and up a broad staircase to the office of Professor Covington. Ivy had scheduled a meeting to meet with her Teacher's Assistant, Tricia. The doors were left open for her.

Ivy was hard on herself to achieve. She had hardly any use for mathematics anymore, and consistently scored high and aced every class. The challenge of antiquity and the constant debate combined with a lack of knowledge of the past fueled her ambitions and drive for perfection these days. She was a perpetual student, who had more than enough credit hours to graduate. She just wanted to stay in class until she figured out exactly what to do with her life. Right now the path was leading her to archaeology.

Ivy walked up one flight then turned and climbed another set of steps to a hallway lined with offices. All were framed by old treated wood. Covington's office lay ahead a few doors on the right. Ivy reached the door when she heard a muffled conversation.

"Don't tell me what I can and can't do! This is my research!" A guttural, gravelly male voice yelled.

"You are making yourself sick. You can't continue like this." Tricia's voice was calmer than the man's, yet trembled.

"I told you! Do not tell me what to do! I will do as I please! You won't stop me! Neither will he!"

"Listen and just look at yourself! You're not yourself!" Tricia's voice shook with fear.

Ivy heard a loud crack, like a big book being pulled by gravity to the old floor. Ivy's heart beat faster. Covington's door was ajar. She pushed her way in. To her left was a series of rooms with open doorways. "Tricia must be in one of these," Ivy thought.

She heard another loud noise. This time it was followed by someone gagging. Ivy froze and peeked out from behind the door. Tricia smashed into the wall closest to the hallway. Someone had thrown her. Tricia lay motionless and her head drooped to her chest. Ivy pulled back and into hallway. She fumbled for the cellphone in her backpack to call the police. She heard footsteps bounding from inside the office toward the door she had just exited. Ivy stopped fumbling for her backpack and ran across the hallway. She prayed someone had left their office unlocked.

The first one she tried opened, and she stepped into a random office. She didn't close the door all the way as to not make any noise. She crouched under a desk. The heavy footfalls resounded in the hallway; they were coming towards the office where Ivy hid.

She heard the door creak open. She figured the person was scanning the room for someone, anyone. The person was in the room with her. He wasn't making a sound, but Ivy could sense a presence. The feeling seemed to last forever. Then she heard the door to her safe haven office shut. Heavy steps headed down the hall way towards the stairs. She peeked over the top of the desk. There was no one in sight.

Terrified, Ivy ran into Covington's office and down the hallway to Tricia. She was immobile and her chin was pinned to her chest. Blood dripped down on the wall behind her. The force of the throw must have cause a severe contusion to the back of her head. Ivy fished her phone from her backpack and called an ambulance.

9

COVINGTON CALLING

Bert, Bud, and Maeve returned to Bud's grandfather's home. They had dragged a panting Maeve to the basement. The damage the ghost of Al Capone had doled out was quite severe.

"This is most concerning, Maeve. When you return to your human undead form there will be considerably more damage to your tissue. Since your cells will not technically be in a live state, there will be no way to heal you without trying to keep you in a live state with a beating heart. This would pump the blood with the necessary antibodies to fight off infection." Bud examined her back which had suffered the greatest wounds. Deep gashes from the ramming bar of the squad car marked Maeve's furry back. Bud kept pressure on some of the wounds while Bert stitched her up.

"My medical protocols have come in quite handily, I might add. What form of the supernatural attacked you Maeve?" Bert sewed up the smaller lacerations, best he could. The large gashes would take considerably more work.

Maeve's muffled vocal box eked and growled out the word, "Poltergeist."

Bert processed the information and searched the internet wirelessly via an antenna in his head.

"A ghost with the ability to interact with the physical world and inflict damage upon the living. I would say that this definition is most accurate," Bert said.

Bud chimed in, "The larger wound's blood will coagulate when dawn hits in a few hours. She will need new blood when we get her back to a live state, which reminds me... Bert did the wire transfer from Ms. Covington come through yet?"

Bert looked up from Maeve's back. She growled as the sudden stitching stoppage hurt her.

"I believe so, but the dollar amount didn't reach the amount needed to purchase more of the equipment needed for a successful attempt at Maeve's reanimation."

Bud's phone vibrated from the insular pocket of his black leather jacket. Bud reached into his jacket and brought out his phone. "Speak of the devil."

Bud cleared his throat.

"Greetings, Mrs. Covington. How may I assist you?"

"I need your help again Mr. Hutchins." Mrs. Covington's smoke-affected voice sounded through the phone's receiver.

"It would appear so. I assumed the evidence we submitted to you was sufficient to prove your husband's infidelity." Bud paced the basement floor, stepping on the green tiles only.

"His mistress has just been murdered in his office. One can only assume the police will be coming to interview my husband. As far as I know, you and I are the only people who know of the affair, so they should not suspect me. I need you to help prove my husband's innocence."

"Wait! You didn't kill Ms. Pazinski did you?"

"No, no of course not. I have no idea who did. The sad part is how crushed my husband is. He must have really loved her." Her voice trembled.

"Were you with your husband this evening? The whole of the evening?"

"Yes, yes. We went to our favorite pizza place and I was pretending everything was normal. Have not brought myself to filing for the divorce papers... I just don't want him to go to jail."

"If he was with you the whole of the evening, he should have a legitimate alibi. My service may not be needed." Bud shook his head since he could really use the money.

"There is one more thing..." Mrs. Covington sighed and paused.

"Yes, what is it my dear?" Bud asked. His brow furrowed. He continued to walk-- the green tiles.

"I sent her a series of text messages saying I knew about the affair and that I would ruin her career."

"So this is not about your husband. This is about proving your innocence. The police have her mobile phone and will search through it. Now I may be of assistance. I can do a simultaneous investigation. My assistant, Bert, will be able to procure any documents the CPD acquires. We have access to every major system in the world. In the meantime, procure a lawyer. Your husband will know that you know when the police arrive. Right now you are a suspect. Depending on the conviction requirements set by the City you may be in trouble."

"That is why I am calling my crack private investigator. Shit, the police are here."

"I will commence with my investigation promptly."

"Thank you Bud. I already doubled your last fee and sent it to you. Keep in touch." Mrs. Covington ended the call.

"Well, Bert, it appears we now have the necessary funds to reanimate our dear friend Maeve." Bud walked over to a closet. He reached for a book on the shelf. He pulled it down and blew the dust off the cover. The book was old and leather-bound. The side of the book was titled, "The Diary of Victor von Frankenstein."

10

FLOATING INVESTIGATION

Bud Hutchins had left a destination marker near the Museum of Science and Industry for sentimental reasons. It was one of the favorite places he and his Grandfather frequented with much regularity, especially in Bud's formative years. He teleported to the lawn in front of the huge marble staircase near the parking garage entrance. The Archaeology Institute was only a few blocks away. The late winter/early spring air held a chill near Lake Michigan. Bud popped the collar of his leather jacket. He stopped to look at the Museum and smiled. The lights on the green dome provided a great deal of warmth to Bud on a chilly night. His Grandfather had understood him best and much of their relationship was spent walking the halls of the grand old building that was once housed the Fine Arts exhibition for the Chicago World's Fair in 1893.

His phone vibrated in his interior breast pocket.

"Bert. Yes. I only left you a minute ago. What could you possibly be in need of?"

Bert's voice rattled through the receiver. "Bud, I just wanted to let you know I found the phone call that pointed the police to the top floor of the Institute and the scene of Ms Pazinski's grisly murder..."

"Bert, out with it. Why must you overuse the pregnant pause when information is vital?"

"The number is registered to an Ivy Zheng, a student at CMU. She lives on campus in Oxford Hall. Her dormitory is number 344. It is highly likely she will still be with the police."

"Excellent. Inform when you have reviewed the surveillance footage in the Institute."

"Working on that now."

"Good." Bud ended the call.

He walked towards the Archaeology Institute. There was Chicago Met University Hospital in front of him. To the left of the hospital, were the Oxford-inspired buildings aplomb with gothic spires, much like Talbot Castle in Wales where Maeve and Bud visited last Autumn.

Bud could see the Institute ahead. There were still CPD squad cars in front of the large wooden doors. The typical yellow tape across the doorway. Bud had anticipated the busy nature of the crime scene. He pulled from his other jacket pocket, a smaller version of a drone he had used earlier. Under cover of night, he could easily use the drone without having to employ the battery-draining cloak function. Bud held the drone up in his left hand and used his right to trigger its start with his phone. The whisper-quiet propellers rotated and lifted the drone from Bud's hand. He raised it and used the night vision of the camera to see the way. He flew it high above the squad cars. Bud sat on a bench then hunched over to concentrate on flight, maintaining stealth, but also hoped to manage enough visual fidelity to get as much info on the murder as he possibly could. The layout of the building that Bert and he had viewed before he arrived on campus, showed there were a series of windows, albeit small windows, in almost every office.

The drone reached the exterior of the top floor of the three-storied Institute. Bud made it strafe the sides of the building. The drone's cam showed a window. He flew it closer. No light was emitting. He moved it to the next window. Still no light. He moved the drone further down. The night vision cam of the drone now bore bright light. Bud adjusted the settings on his phone from night vision to normal vision mode. The lights were on. He moved the drone closer to the window. About 15 feet away on the opposite wall was a blood streak, above the body of Tricia Pazinski. Bud zoomed in to get as many photos as he could.

Bud kept the drone in a stable hover. From the pictures on the screen of his phone, he surmised that Tricia was beaten to death. There were no visible signs of any stab wounds. The office space between her body and the window was filled with papers, an open file cabinet, and a tray with artifacts that had spilled on the floor. Ms. Pazinski had put up a fight with whomever savagely dispensed with her life.

Bud knew he would have to get in and examine the scene much more thoroughly. He moved the drone back to the stone windowsill of an office with no lights on, spun the drone around 180 degrees and hit an icon within the drone app that said "payload." A destination marker dropped from underbelly of the drone. Bud flew the drone back to where he sat. He stood up and grabbed it. With the drone secured to his jacket pocket, he walked past the squad cars and around to the office windows. He readied his teleportation wristband. A risky but not impossible use of his teleportation tech played out in his mind. A murder investigation meant that time was always the enemy; Bud needed to get into the offices unseen.

11

WINDOWING

Bud's phone buzzed. It was Bert. "I see you activated a destination marker on a windowsill. The likelihood of that succeeding is rather, well, unlikely."

"We have no time for debate Bert. The new markers are pinpointed to my feet. I shall succeed in the endeavor by balancing and securing the rest of my person with my hands on the window frame."

"Bud, Maeve thinks this a fool's move as well," Bert said.

"I assume you were able to get her to a stable undead state?" Bud asked.

"The moon is still full and she is in wolf form. She has been stitched and wrapped with great care. I don't want to employ the same medic subroutines on you when you fall from the windowsill, unable to recover successfully from your teleportation."

"Nonsense, it will work." Bud ended the phone call. He stared at the third story of the Institute and found the darkened window where he dropped the marker. Bud flailed his arms to warm up for grabbing the window frame. He had done it several times over. Bud took a deep breath then exhaled and cocked his head, pretending he was a formidable physical presence and not a wiry, lanky young man. With his legs shoulder-length apart, he initiated teleportation on his wristband.

Bud found himself on the windowsill. His feet were partially planted but soon uprooted. He flailed his arms hoping to catch the window frame. Bud's hands scraped the glass window. He wished so desperately that the tips of fingers were like that of an arachnid's and would stick. Instead, they helped propel his backwards fall off the small ledge. The shock of falling overwhelmed Bud and he could not bring himself to teleport his way out of the dire situation. The third story was high enough to do major damage, but also too short a distance to actually react accordingly. Bud opened his eyes wide and hoped his inevitable incapacitation would be short and manageable.

Just as Bud figured his short trip would come to an end, he saw his teleportation wristband light up.

Bud's felt a soft cushion give way to the springs of his twin bed that coiled underneath him. The metal frame of his bed collapsed.

"Holy shit." Bud dropped his fake English accent in times of distress.

He did not move. He looked around at the spare bedroom of his Grandfather's home. The walls were off-white.

There were old movie posters decorating the walls, some framed, some tacked on to the wall. Stacks of VHS tapes on a shelf and he could not have felt happier to be home. He lay and stared at the 1980s physical media.

Bert entered the room. "You are welcome Bud."

Bud recovered quickly upon seeing Bert and readied his defense. "It will work. The night blocked my perception of how much room I actually had in the window frame. You will get no thanks from me. I did not ask that you remotely initiate teleportation."

"Even if it was to safety, sir?" Bert asked.

"I still need to investigate the Institute. Again, only call me when you have the surveillance information."

Bud teleported back to the grounds of the Museum of Science and Industry. He did not want to tell Bert, his android assistant, that he had been right. Pride that was grossly impregnable to any criticism made Bud friendless. He only had become acquainted with Maeve when he had investigated her Uncle's death.

He would revise his strategy: visit Oxford Hall and hope that Ivy Zheng was done answering questions and filing reports with the police.

12

CONCENTRATED EBB
AND FLOW

The single light bulb swung back and forth in the small room. The glass beakers had been replaced. A few shards from their predecessors still glistened from the floor in the yellow glow of the bulb.

The huddled man sat on a stool with his head in his hands. That idiot Covington only had a partial understanding of what needed to be done. His emphasis on physical components in a solid state had been his folly. The chemical nature of the research still seemed lost to the tenured Archaeology professor. This frustrated the man more and more with each passing day. The deadline approached and the Board still favored Covington over him. This bias was not official but the egregiously gracious nature of their be-havior towards Covington enraged him.

Still he must push on. He'll try the mixture again with this new material. He felt he was close and a calm washed over him when he focused solely on his work. He prepped his lab for another experiment. His work would be considered revolutionary and would change the world. He took solace in the dreams of his victory, no matter the means of his accomplishment. The end-game would bring him glory and frankly, no one would be able to stop him from success once he found the right mixture. A rare smile adorned his face, not borne of happiness, but of visceral dominance. It was a smile that a fierce competitor employs to mock a fallen foe.

13

BUD MEETS IVY

Oxford Hall had a gothic bell tower spire similar to other buildings on campus yet that was the only similarity. It also had a redesigned front adorned with panes of glass and a modern look, similar in nature to Soldier Field in Chicago where architectural contrast is on full display. The stadium that was once purely Greco-Roman now had a modern glass bowl around its interior. It jutted over the stone columns in places as if a spaceship had landed in it but couldn't quite fit. Bud shook his head as he approached the dormitory. He checked his phone and scrolled through the long text message thread from Bert. He had sent him Ivy's information including door codes after he informed Bud of her call to the police.

He entered Oxford Hall. A security guard sat a desk. Bud casually walked past the security guard who was watching a video on his phone.

The upgrade to electronic keypad locks made Bud's life much easier. Bud used a camera filter on his phone to scan the keypad for its model number and the most likely lock combinations. Bud's camera gave him actionable intel, door keypads of this model, usually had a six-digit combo with the first three digits being the same and then varying after that. Through the filter Bud could see glowing fingerprints which were the most concentrated on digits 2, 5, and 7. He entered that combination then remembered Bert told him Ivy's room number 344. It worked. The door lock opened.

"This system is incredibly stupid. Parents of students should be bursting with lividity," Bud thought.

He entered a hall with elevators to the left and a stairwell on the right. He chose to wait for the elevator. A group of students spilled out of the elevator, and Bud quickly covered his nose and mouth with his sleeve. Hypochondria. The students smelled of booze. They each held laptops and components of a computer to assemble it for a night of intense PC gaming. Chicago Met was not your typical party school.

Bud was glad the elevator was empty. He used his sleeve to hit the button for the third floor. The elevator moved swiftly. 344 was to his right. He knocked on the door. A young, thin Chinese woman with black-rimmed glasses opened the door.

"Ivy, I presume." Bud held his P.I. License in the air. The one that Officer Hanks scoffed at the autumn before in Salem.

"Ugh, I just got done talking to the police. I want to be left alone! I just told them I don't want any counsel. I just want to be alone. Leave me alone." She slammed the door in Bud's face.

Bud knocked again and said, "I can help find the killer much faster than the cops can. Alas, we need to converse in order to fulfill my audacious claim."

Ivy opened the door; her logic and curiosity drove her. "Who are you? How did you know to come here?"

"I am Bud Hutchins. I am a private investigator working for Mrs. Covington, the wife of your professor. It was his teacher's assistant, Tricia who was so viciously murdered. In order to clear my client, I need your help."

She examined Bud's license, his weak stature, and eyes. She shut the door in his face again.

Bud shook his head.

She opened the door with her backpack on her shoulder.

"Let's go. Tricia was my friend. I will help in any way I can." She locked her door. Ivy bumped into Bud as she brushed ahead of him back toward the elevator. Bud was actually flustered and somewhat intimidated.

"Can you get us into the Institute past the police tape?" Bud asked.

"I know another way in."

14

NO EXIT

Ivy and Bud headed back to the Institute. Ivy brought Bud around the building to a set of stairs that led underground to the basement of the Institute. The police had not even thought to block this area off with the procedural caution tape. The steps were dirty; the ambient light from the city helped guide Ivy and Bud down to a door.

"I didn't want anyone to know that I know about this door. Technically, no one uses it, but the maintenance team," Ivy said.

"Why the secrecy?" Bud inquired.

"I come down here to study the artifacts stored here. Tricia did not know I would sneak in. Earlier I had an appointment with her and she left the front doors open for me. That is when I saw what happened. It was brutal and loud. We have to find out who did this." Ivy opened the door with a special padlock key.

She moved with a forward momentum so pronounced that even the hyperactive Bud Hutchins was reeling.

"Do you think it wise to move so quickly? The murderer could be sequestered in the basement. Perhaps we should employ a slower gait."

"I did hear heavy footfalls run away and down the stairs to the lobby. I wonder if the cops checked the camera footage yet? I suppose you are right. You said you had resources available to you so why haven't you checked yet?"

Ivy opened the door and stamped her feet. She then flipped a switch which caused a fluorescent wave of lights; some blinked on while others pulsed with power. The basement of the Institute had row upon row of casing and labels, shelves, and trays, all marked with numbers of a Dewey decimal system.

"Well, so much for a stealthy approach." Bud slapped his forehead.

"If the killer is in here, lights help make him or her easier to find," Ivy said.

"Right, right. Let me...let me check with Bert. He was supposed to have been compiling the necessary surveillance footage."

Bert called Bud.

"Speak of the devil. Yes, Bert," Bud said.

The robotic voice burst from the speaker of Bud's phone. Ivy listened intently.

"I have accessed the footage. A hooded figure dressed darkly runs down the stairs to the lobby of the Institute but does not leave out the front door. The figure heads into the gallery of the Institute," Bert said.

"I have been freshly made privy to another door around the back or south end of the building. It is a basement door at the base of a stairwell. The hooded figure may have exited via that door. Any cameras near the south end of the building?"

"Yes, of course, I scanned every camera around the building. The only footage bearing any person that is not Ms. Ivy, was the hooded figure that headed into the gallery."

"Peruse the footage again," Bud said.

"No need to sir. My hard drive is solid state. My memory is locked down. Checking things twice is only derived from the mistakes of humanity. I am no human Bud. You designed me that way."

Bud shook his head. He knew Bert was right. In a way, Bud wanted Bert to be wrong because of the windowsill incident.

"So the killer is still in this building and somehow eluded the police search of the building."

"It appears to be so Bud," Bert said.

Ivy interjected: "Enough talk. Let's find this asshole."

15

ILLUSORY INSTITUTION

Bud followed Ivy into the rows of artifacts.

"I assure you the police would have found the culprit by the present time," Bud said.

"Like they cordoned off the basement door?" Ivy retorted.

"Your point is most astutely taken." Bud watched as she crouched down and looked below some of the long tables. "Bert told us of the hooded figure entering the gallery perhaps we should check there first."

"How do we get up there without being seen? I am sure the cops have the area blocked off by now and the doors locked," Ivy asked.

"You granted us entry to the basement. Now let me work. This means your pace must be more controlled and slowed Ms. Zheng."

"I have been through a lot and I don't need a lecture from a sleazy private investigator." Her face was visibly upset. Her brow wrinkled above her black rim glasses.

"I am not lecturing. It would be better if we worked together instead of exacting futile levels of inertia on each other." Bud missed Maeve, his original female companion in a similar situation. She was more patient with him.

Bud called Bert, "Has the CPD removed the body yet?"

"Yes Bud. They brought her out eight minutes ago. The police are patrolling the area heavily and campus security will be on duty in the Institute the rest of the evening. It would be wise to use a stealthier approach." Bud looked at Ivy and knew she could hear Bert's advice.

She shrugged.

"Thank you, Bert." Bud ended the call and headed towards the stairwell that led to the lobby.

"You can't just walk up the stairs if campus security is on watch," Ivy said.

"I am not walking up the stairs to my capture. I am positioning myself for our entry into the gallery."

Bud stopped at the base of the stairwell. He brought out the mini-drone from his leather jacket pocket and his phone. He initiated the flight control. The drone hovered, whisper-quiet. He initiated the cloak. The battery drained substantially but the drone would not have to fly far. Bud could see the lobby desk through the drone's camera. Two campus security guards in white and blue uniforms sat at the desk, talking. Neither seemed to be doing or attempting to be doing any rounds.

The doors to the gallery were set back to the left of the desk. The gallery's lights were off.

"One would think they would leave the lights on," Bud commented.

"If you said the cops searched everywhere then there is no need to have the lights on. Plus, light damages some of the art pieces in the gallery," Ivy said.

"I am aware of light damage, but this is certainly an exceptional evening."

"What are you planning to do with the drone? It's impressive you made it disappear. I will admit it."

Bud flew the drone up the stairwell leading from the lobby towards the scene of the crime. He turned the camera towards the guards. Their conversation was engaging. Bud then pressed an orange icon on the screen of his phone. The drone began to click.

SNIK! SNIK! SNIK!

The guards looked towards the ascending stairs then at each other.

One yelled, "What the fuck was that?"

"Probably nothing. Don't worry about it."

Bud pressed the orange button over and over again. The drone was farther up the stairs.

SNIK! SNIK! SNIK! SNIK! SNIK!

"Okay we should check it out!"

"This place has to be haunted. What the shit?"

Ivy and Bud heard the rolling wheels of a chair, then two sets of footsteps moving towards the upper stairwell. The long strides of a walk turned to short hops of climbing stairs.

Bud piloted the drone all the way to end of the office hallway and pressed the orange button a few more times. He moved the drone into an office, dropped the mini-drone into a garbage can, and turned off the cloak.

"Now is our time to move."

Bud climbed the stairs. The guards were in pursuit of his phantom drone. The way to the gallery doors was clear.

"What if the gallery doors are locked?" Ivy was right behind Bud.

"That is of no matter. I need you to wear this." Bud brought out a wristband.

Ivy secured the band to her narrow wrist. Bud pulled a marker from his pocket and slid it under the double door.

"I think you will find this ever more impressive than a cloaked drone." Bud smiled.

16

GHOULISH GALLERY

"I shall go into the gallery first then I will activate your wristband."

Bud pulled back his black leather sleeve to reveal a similar band to the one Bud had just given Ivy. He suddenly disappeared. She was listening to the guards clearing the various offices upstairs when she realized that she was no longer in the lobby but in the gallery. She turned around to see the lights of the lobby through the glass double doors of the interior of the Babylonian gallery. Her nerves were rattled. She was shaking from the sudden shift through space she had experienced. Adrenaline pumped through her veins at a quickening pace and her heart pounded.

"You are officially the first student of Chicago Met to have teleported. Certainly, there must be no equal to that distinction in the annals of this great institution.

Now gather yourself. We must find Ms. Tricia Pazinski's murderer."

Bud brought up the camera on his phone. He activated the flashlight and a list of different filters for three-dimensional space. A thermal camera, a motion detector, and fingerprint scanner-- the very same tech he used to enter Ivy's dormitory.

"How? Is this possible?" Ivy asked looking towards Bud's face softly illuminated by the phone's flashlight.

"Certainly you can surmise various theories on how I was able to accomplish teleportation but I will spare you the details. We must press our advantage and figure out where this hooded figure is."

"I mean I understand how you are able to break down your molecular mass but how do you transport and rebuild it in a different space? How did you do this?" Ivy's innate curiosity sparked. She became ravenous for answers.

"Ivy, if I tell you then the novelty would wear off. I cannot reveal too much especially to someone of your intellect. It will not be contained, nor would my patent for it be my own. I hope you understand my need for safeguarding my technology. Now we must stick to the sides of the gallery behind the cabinets so as to not arouse the guards' suspicion upon their return to the lobby."

Bud moved off the main walkway and in between two large show cabinets. He scanned the area for the culprit.

Ivy followed Bud shaking her head in disbelief. Respect for Bud began to grow. Perhaps he was not a typical private investigator who chased adulterers and people who stole credit card numbers from gas stations.

"I don't think her murderer would be hiding in this corner of pottery shards and demon figurines," Ivy said.

Bud scanned the glass cabinet. Ivy was not wrong. Shards and small figurines. One figure of which had a human body, a dog's head, and two pairs of large wings.

"Oh, dear, that is Pazuzu. Is it not?" Bud asked.

"Yes. A Babylonian demon associated with rain and drought. Inherently evil but also a champion against other evil spirits and the nemesis of Lamashtu, the demon that attacks pregnant woman," Ivy said.

"Hmm, keeps evil spirits at bay not unlike the Order of St. Michael..." Bud said.

"What's that? Anyway, Pazuzu is associated with horror films and people don't focus on the good efforts of the demon. Pregnant women would keep a figurine of Pazuzu in their home to keep away Lamashtu."

"Sounds perfectly logical..." Bud couldn't believe he had said that. His experiences with Maeve and the Order had been slowly turning him away from always thinking there is a scientific, practical reason for everything.

"...yet ludicrous." Bud finished. He still had a way to go even after all he had gone through. He moved on to the next section of the gallery and perhaps the most impressive.

"We are heading towards the giant Assyrian King Sargon relief. The one thing that might be of note is that the relief is not flush to the wall. There is a backside to it.

Be careful. It is a pretty good hiding spot especially given how careless the cops were on their initial search," Ivy said.

Bud shined his cell light on the large stone raised relief section of a palace wall. The relief depicted King Sargon combined with a beast that had five legs and hooves for feet. Bud was impressed with the craftsmanship. He stepped closer to the ancient stone grey wall and slowly moved to the side to light the back of the wall.

Ivy followed Bud. She kept both hands on his back and peeked over his shoulder. Bud lifted his phone to eye level and initiated a thermal scan. The space behind the relief, which was only about a three-feet wide, showed a slight reading.

Bud and Ivy moved closer to the space. He looked at the screen of his phone. Ivy looked at what the phone's flashlight showed.

"There is no one there Bud," Ivy whispered.

Bud looked up from the screen of his thermal imaging app. "It appears to be so, yet someone may have rested here. I am still seeing a slight thermal signature."

POP!

Ivy jumped on Bud's back. He nearly lost his balance. One of the track lights that illuminated the writing above the rear of the relief had broken.

"A faulty light bulb! Even with the lights off, a loose wire can still carry a charge. It could have merely loosened from a poor job at screwing the bulb in. The wiring in this old building must not be to code. Anyway, what does this writing say?" Bud asked.

Ivy slid off Bud's back.

"Sorry about that. It is just the typical boasting of the king's greatness. His biography and achievements are written here but not necessarily for the purpose of being read. Knowing that it has been recorded is what mattered to the Assyrians. They would write on keystones implanted into the ground. It was not important that anyone knew the writing was there," Ivy said.

"How strange the ancient customs were." Bud turned away from the Assyrian gallery and headed to the next section. They had to make a right turn as the layout of the entire gallery was a U shape.

They heard the sound of something heavy, like a large piece of furniture, being dragged on the marble floor. It came from somewhere ahead of Ivy and Bud.

"One can assume the custodial staff does not respond that quickly to broken light vessels. What is the content of the next gallery?"

"The Egyptian mummies," Ivy said.

17

MUMMIFIED REMAINS

Bud and Ivy pushed farther into the Archaeological Institute's world famous gallery. The sound of rolling wheels ceased. Bud turned his phone's flashlight function off. He brought up the night vision filter.

Ivy knew the gallery backwards and forwards.

"A fourteen-foot statue of King Tut marks the entrance to the Egyptian section," Ivy whispered.

Bud moved the screen of his phone and saw the cobra headdress of King Tutankhamen colored green by the night vision filter. He and Ivy moved around the statue and into the Egyptian section. Bud switched quickly to the motion sensor app. A few feet into the gallery something moved. The reading on his phone marked a slight three out of a possible ten rating. He kept the phone aimed in the exact same spot as the movement. Nothing.

Bud checked the night vision screen and only saw a square box approximately six by six foot in size. Then he quickly switched back to the thermal app. Again nothing. It could have been a rat or some other critter taking refuge underneath the large square display case.

"No one is there. I think it safe to use the flashlight again. Let's examine this box over here." Bud said.

"This is an Old Kingdom burial display. Look at how this person was mummified in the fetal position. Most Egyptians were buried in this way. Only the royals and upper class could afford the ornate and detailed sarcophagus burial," Ivy said.

Bud examined the mummy. It's carbon-colored exterior and brittle bones both fascinated Bud and gave him a slight chill considering the situation he and Ivy were in, searching for a killer among corpses. The small resting place the mummy had was both comforting but also terribly claustrophobic. Around the mummy's body were pottery shards and other things that this fellow needed for his sojourn into the afterlife. Bud's close examination of the body caused the square burial display case to move and reproduce the same grinding sound that had prompted their investigation of the area.

"Bud you moved it!" Ivy said.

"It appears to be so."

Bud dropped to the floor and flashed the light underneath the case. There was a small two-inch separation between the case and the tiles. This case could be moved and swapped out easily. It had wheels underneath it.

"Ivy, we must examine what is under this case. Help me push it."

Bud stood up and Ivy assisted him with moving the case about six feet away from its original spot.

"That was easier than I expected," Ivy said.

"Indeed, I am not known for my physical prowess," Bud added.

"Unequivocally not." Ivy mimicked Bud's fake English accent.

Bud shone the flashlight on the floor. There was a panel with a depressed handle. Bud grabbed it expecting it to lift.

"Oh poppycock. I can't be that weak," Bud said.

"You might actually be that weak," Ivy said.

Bud's grip on the handle started to move the panel. It did not raise, it actually slid over the floor revealing a dark passage.

"Perhaps we have the reason for Trish's murderer's prompt run into the gallery-- an underground passage. I am all too familiar with subterranean environs. I was almost sacrificed to a pagan god in one." Bud ignored Ivy's last jab.

Ivy's intense focus caused her to be apathetic to Bud's past plight. Her friend was murdered. She wanted to find the killer now.

"I really don't need to hear a story right now. It is almost morning. Are we going down or what? We have to make it back up here if the Institute opens or should we just send for the police?" Ivy asked.

"I prefer not having to explain myself to the police. I will most certainly be shackled for my sarcasm and condescending tone."

Bud shined the light down into the passage. There was a small ladder descending to a stone floor. He lowered himself down and Ivy followed.

There was a long corridor in front of them. Gothic light fixtures that looked as if they were converted from gas to electric, provided dim light along the walls. The floor was haphazardly cobbled together with brick and mortar.

Ivy stepped off the ladder to the uneven ground.

"Shall we?" Bud motioned towards the long corridor.

"We shall." Ivy took a deep breath and walked ahead of Bud.

Bud's phone buzzed. Bert said: "Maeve and I have surmised another possible sighting of our poltergeist along Archer Avenue. The police and emergency scanner indicates a few auto crashes throughout the night on a forest preserve road. All reported a female hitchhiker as the cause."

"Clever poltergeist, assuming the forms of Chicago legends Al Capone and now Resurrection Mary. She is rumored to have died in an accident along Archer Avenue in the 1930s. Since then she has haunted drivers using said avenue. I would start your investigation around Resurrection Cemetery near the grave which many ghost hunters claim is the remains of Mary. Then make your way down the road. How is Maeve? Back in undead form?"

"She is no longer the beast and her wounds from the grill of the squad car are stitched and holding. I have since ordered the remaining components for our restorative experiment. They will be delivered shortly. Spared no expense," Bert said.

"Excellent. Ivy and I remain ever vigilant on the hunt for our killer. Keep me apprised of the resurrection of Resurrection Mary." Bud ended the call and followed Ivy down the old, underground tunnel on the path of a cold-blooded killer.

18

LAB OF RENOWN

The corridor seemed to go on forever with no entrances or exits anywhere. No offshoots, nooks, or crannies surprised them. It was a long march. They were at least a mile from the Institute.

"This is crazy. Is there no end to this!" Ivy exclaimed.

"Perhaps it would be wise to not yell," Bud said.

They kept on down the path. It felt humid in the tunnel. There was a smell that emanated from further down the tunnel. They hadn't smelled anything until this point.

"Smells like a Bunsen burner," Ivy observed.

The end of the line seemed near. The dim lamps that lit the path showed a grey steel door on the right wall of the tunnel, like the kind found in a submarine. A hatch mechanism stood between Ivy and Bud and entry into the only room they had found along the corridor.

The smell of a recently used Bunsen burner grew stronger.

Bud used his phone to examine for fingerprints. There were many, but all seemed to be concentrated in the same spots on the hatch handles which most likely meant that only one person had used this room in the past few hours.

"The door is too thick and made of steel so my thermal camera won't work. We will just have to open it and see who or what is inside. Be ready. I may have to teleport us out of here should danger strike. Stand to the side."

Bud grasped the hatch handles and pulled clockwise. He grimaced but was able to open the door. Ivy stood ready to pounce on whomever was in the room. They both froze and looked at each other. They could be facing someone willing to beat a woman to death. Ivy and Bud nodded to each other and simultaneously entered the room.

The room was a laboratory. A single lightbulb descending from a wire attached to the ceiling showed a table with the Bunsen burner, beakers, a microscope. The room was much bigger than the light indicated. No signs of life in the room either.

"This couldn't be what I think it is..." Bud said.

"What are you thinking?"

"The labs where Chicago Met helped to develop the atomic bomb."

"You may be right. It's big enough for a team of scientists. This is strange." Ivy examined the table under the lightbulb.

"This whole night has been strange. Thankfully, the sun will be up shortly. What have you got?"

"There are artifacts all over this table. Pottery, figurines, tablets, even some cylinder seals. They've all been shaved or heated. Broken down in some way. Chipped away..." She picked up a bowl that had powder in it that had been ground from various artifacts from the Institute. "Why destroy ancient artifacts from the Institute?"

"Perhaps they have some properties while in another form?" Bud asked.

"Maybe. I should take sample of this. I was a chem major before I turned to Archaeology."

"You don't seem the type to be decisive. A career student I presume." Bud picked up a cylinder seal.

"You really are a jerk aren't you? If we want to do this right, this will take some time. Maybe you should collect some evidence with your phone while I actually try and figure out what the hell is going on," Ivy said.

"Gather what you need. I shall examine the lab further."

Bud picked up a book on the floor next the table of artifacts. It was a history book. It had bookmarks jutting from various sections. He opened to the first one. Inside were notes. One scribble pointing to a spot on the map between the Tigris and Euphrates rivers read, "The origin of the Elixir".

He showed the book to Ivy. "Perhaps these artifacts are needed to make this? An elixir of the ancients as it were?"

19

BLOCKADE AND BEEPER

Bert and Maeve finally reached Archer Avenue after making a considerable trek through many traffic lights all the way down 79th street. Traffic was light as the sun was just beginning to peek over the eastern horizon. Maeve stared at the sky. She remembered her early morning hikes with her Uncle through the forests of New England. Those were simpler, happier times.

Her Uncle was a caring yet demanding man. Her long hikes were lessons in discipline and sacrifice for her training in The Order of St. Michael. Maeve did not live the life of a typical American teenager. No smartphone. No game consoles. No frequent shopping jaunts. She lived a life of sworn poverty. The life of a monk.

"It is indeed strange that all these auto accidents occurred in the same evening. Is it not Maeve?" Bert's conversation protocol kicked in every 15 minutes.

"It has to be the poltergeist from Mt. Olivet taking the form of another Chicago legend. The monks of the Order in Chicago have certainly been sealing their trees every night. This ghost followed us from Llanwelly," Maeve responded with the same voice as Bert.

"Have you any contact with the Chicago members of the Order?" Bert asked while driving the speed limit along the forested roads of Archer Avenue, just outside the city limits.

"When we settled in Bud's house, I alerted them with our secret pager system that I was in Chicago. Other than that, there has been no contact, but that is normal for a hermit Order. If we do hear from them then serious shit is hitting the fan."

"Pager? I am sorry what does shit have to do with it?"

"A pager or beeper from the early 90s. A form of wireless communication...just google it in your head. Bud needs to update your slang database. Up ahead must be an accident site."

Two squad cars' lights spun as a tow truck hauling a wrecked crossover SUV drove towards Bert and Maeve.

"Drive on. Further down the road. Maybe we will see our hitchhiker."

They made it another hundred yards when they noticed the squad cars formed a blockade. They closed Archer. The morning commute would be rough for many workers emerging from sleep.

Bert drove to the blockade when a cop signaled for him to turn around. Bert kept driving forward.

"What seems to be the problem officer?" Bert said as he rolled his window down. An officer walked to the car.

"We have had a rash of accidents. People seriously hurt. We have an inspection team checking the road for potholes and whatnot. Please turn around." The young police officer put his hands on his hips.

"Thank you officer. We shall take another route to our destination." Bert stared at the officer.

"Okay move along now. Let's go." The officer shooed him away.

"Bert!" Maeve urged Bert to turn around and drive.

Bert finally made a move.

"You are so awkward," Maeve said. "We had better find a way onto Archer even if it is on foot. If there really is a road inspection team they are in grave danger."

"I believe there is a short parallel street to Archer that ends in a small residential neighborhood. We can park there then traverse on foot."

Bert turned off Archer and onto La Grange Road south to the next light and the parallel road.

Maeve heard a beeping sound. If she could properly feel anything her heart would have dropped. She grabbed the pager from her hoodie. The Order needed help.

"Shit!" Maeve illuminated the green LED screen of the obsolete device.

"Is this where serious shit hits a fan?" Bert asked as he parked the car in the residential neighborhood.

"Yes Bert. I need you to trace the number now." She held the pager in front of Bert's face.

He scanned the number. "It is from a landline in a St. James of the Sag Church just down Archer Avenue past the blockade."

"Oh no. Let's go Bert! A monk needs our help!"

"Walking will take around 45 minutes."

"I am a zombie! It will take me forever. I can barely walk as it is. We have to break the blockade."

20

BLOCKADE RUN

"I am afraid that my driving protocols restrict me from putting us in any danger and breaking the blockade of municipal police vehicles is very dangerous." Bert stopped next to a gray ranch house in the neighborhood parallel to Archer Avenue.

"I am driving. Move." Maeve opened the passenger door.

"I don't think this wise." Bert put his hands up.

Maeve walked around the car and pulled the driver door open.

"It does not matter what you think. A monk is in danger down the road and that damn inspection team. Now get out." Maeve's artificial vocal chord eked out monotone commands but their content gave her voice a menacing feel, like an evil A.I. voice in a sci-fi film.

Bert exited the car and hopped in the passenger seat.

Maeve slammed her door, best she could with the use of her stiff undead muscles.

The dawn's light hit the street in front of them. Maeve pushed the pedal to the floor. A man emerged to grab his morning paper and barked at her to slow down. She didn't.

"My map application shows no exit from this neighborhood. There is a slight elevation to consider as we are higher up than Archer Avenue. So we will most likely roll the vehicle if we continue on our current route." If Bert could cover his optics he would.

Maeve drove between two homes without backyard fences.

"Beyond this yard is a considerable drop off. I urge you to not continue----" Bert stopped.

The red beater Grand Am rumbled through the backyard and down the hill. Bert's head hit the window then the interior roof of the car. Maeve gripped the steering wheel. The car rumbled down the hill. The morning dew may have helped quicken their descent. It created a slippery surface for the tires to roll down the grassy, muddy hillside. The yellow dashes on Archer Avenue fast approached. Maeve turned the wheel to the left in anticipation of hitting the pavement. The car hit another big bump and Bert flew out of his seat and again hit his head. Maeve applied the brakes again and skidded sideways onto Archer Avenue.

Maeve pumped the brakes. The car stopped facing the proper direction towards St. James of the Sag, home to monk who reached out for help. She pushed down on the accelerator. Maeve looked in the rearview mirror to see the police blockade grow smaller and smaller.

"We did it Bert!" Her robotic voice adulated.

"We have done nothing but jeopardize the safety of ourselves and others," Bert said.

"How much longer 'til we get to the church?" Maeve asked, ignoring his previous comment.

"At the current rate of speed approximately four minutes. Alas, be on the lookout for the road inspection team."

"You mean them?" Maeve pointed towards a team with reflective vests running towards the car about a hundred yards ahead. Three men waved their hands at Maeve and Bert and kept a steady run.

"Bert, you will have to talk with them. Maeve secured her hood over her head. She did not want to scare the already frightened men with her zombie face. She pulled up to the men and slowed the car to a gentle stop. Bert rolled down his window and popped his head out.

"How may we be of assistance?"

"Let us in! Let us in!" The burly man pulled at the back door handle. The two other men gathered behind him, yelling, "Hurry up! She's right there! Fucking Resurrection Mary!"

Maeve looked ahead and in front of the car was a ghostly woman, with the same blue hue as Capone. She wore a party dress commonly worn in the clubs of the Prohibition era. The dress was short. Her hair cropped, yet her bangs hung low across her face blocking her eyes. She walked towards the car. As she moved closer, she lifted her arm in a hitchhiking pose and beckoned for their car to pick her up.

Maeve unlocked the doors. The men still scrambled with the handle.

Resurrection Mary walked closer to the car only a few feet away.

The first man piled into the backseat.

Mary reached the front bumper.

The second man fell into the car. The third man slipped and fell to his knees failing to reach the backseat.

"Back the car up! Back it up! It's too late for Jerry! Go!" The burly man yelled from the backseat.

Maeve refused to move the car. The third man got up and started running into the forest off the right side of the road.

Resurrection Mary walked over to Bert's front passenger door. Her head began to shake. Her bangs receded. The skin melted off her face. Her mouth opened.

Mary's skull caved in on the right side of her skull. Her ghostly tongue hung out of her mouth in a wrangled, serpentine mess. The gore was too much to bear even for Bert. He shut down his optics.

Maeve hit the accelerator, jolting the car forward.

"What are you doing?! Don't go this way! That's what she wants!" The burly man warned.

Maeve drove. She needed to save the monk of the Order at St. James Church. Suddenly, the trees that lined the sides of Archer Avenue began to crack with a splintering, thundering boom. They swayed violently and began to fall on the road ahead.

21

MAEVE AND MARY SITTING IN A TREE...

Maeve drove underneath one of the falling maple trees before it hit the ground, but would not evade the fallen pine that lay in large chunks in front of them. She pushed hard on the brakes. Bert hit his head on the windshield. The two road workers jolted forward and almost landed in Maeve's lap. The car was now essentially trapped between two trees. The pine tree split apart into logs, which then rolled and began to levitate in front of the car. Another tree fell and cracked in front of them. This one did not split into large chunks as the first pine had. Mary did not want Maeve to accelerate. The logs swayed back and forth in the air as if on a pendulum readying to smash through the windshield of Bud's car.

"Everyone get out of the car now!" Maeve urged. Her voice apparatus was strained.

The road workers each jumped through their respective passenger doors and rolled onto the pavement. They ran into the woods away from Resurrection Mary.

Bert exited the vehicle and turned to face Resurrection Mary who was approaching the rear of the vehicle. The remnants of her grotesque ghastly skin hung off her skull and twitched as she moved closer. Bert struggled to look at her.

Maeve stood up out of the car, grasped her crucifix and faced the swaying logs. One of them flew towards Bert, who was still facing Mary. The log smashed into his back and splintered. Bert's metal frame held up, but Maeve's body would not be able to withstand such a blow.

Bert dove headfirst over the hood of the car. Another log swung and spun towards Maeve. He intended on shielding her, but the log burst into flames then shattered just as it was about to crush her head.

"Still got it." Maeve lowered her crucifix. Bert slipped off the hood of the car as he marveled at Maeve's ability to set matter on fire at will. She developed this power in her training with her Uncle to become a monk of the Order of St. Michael.

"Impressive Maeve. Alas, we are not out of the woods yet. Literally."

More trees swayed, creaked, and cracked. Resurrection Mary stood on the street next to passenger side of the car, Maeve and Bert were on the driver side. Mary put her hands on the car and began to push it towards Bert and Maeve. The trees behind them splintered into spears. Trunks jutted from the ground. Pikes, spears, and other impaling shapes formed at their rear and hovered forming a horrendous trap.

"This is most precarious." Bert's head spun around 360 degrees to see the trap.

"Oh dear. Don't ever do that again. In fact, run as fast as you can to St. James and see what happened to the monk. I will handle this bitch," Maeve said.

Resurrection Mary pushed the car closer to the spears that were hovering at the side of the road.

"I shall be off then. Be safe and try not to sustain any more soft tissue damage. Bud is worried you are beyond repair." Bert slid under a tree spear and ran down Archer Avenue.

A spear flew at Maeve. She ducked. The spear smashed through the driver door window. The space between the car and the jutting wooden death dealers slimmed to at least two feet. Maeve reached into the car and grabbed the spear. She secured it between her legs. She hoped that in her undead state, she could still use the power she had absorbed from the witches of Salem- the power of flight.

22

...K-I-L-L-I-N-G

Maeve hopped up and down once. Nothing happened. She grasped the stick and crouched. She prayed. Suddenly, the stick lifted her off the ground. If Maeve could smile, she would have. She quickly flew up and away from the vice-like trap Resurrection Mary had so effortlessly assembled. Maeve ascended to the tops of the trees; Mary looked up and let out a blood-curdling scream. The remaining windows and windshield of Bud' car shattered from the sonic ferocity of a tortured banshee. Mary flipped the car over. This was the same tactic that had caused all of the other accidents throughout the course of the last evening.

Maeve flew over the carnage then readied herself to charge at Mary with the pointed end of the spear turned rocket. Her hands gripped just under the jagged edge.

Resurrection Mary anticipated Maeve's tactical advantage and commanded her broken tree fragments to angle upwards like an anti-air battery from World War 2.

"Not good." Maeve leaned forward and began a fast, but controlled descent towards Resurrection Mary.

The flak in the form of jagged sticks, spears, and blunt wooden objects cut through the chilled morning air and flew towards Maeve. There was no way she would be able to avoid all of it.

A few small jagged sticks peppered Maeve's arms and shoulders. She flew further down and avoided a huge tree trunk that barreled toward her head. She leaned to the left then recovered to center. She maintained a direct path to Mary who was now only a few feet below.

Mary let out another scream. This time her audible angst was cut short as Maeve drove the spear she rode into the belly of the reanimated and corporeal Resurrection Mary. The same general form that the poltergeist assumed after absconding and disturbing the remains of Alphonse Capone.

Maeve lifted Mary off the ground. Mary reeled and gripped the spear in agony. Her disgusting, deathly, decaying face didn't scare Maeve, given her own personal situation at the moment. She flew the impaled Mary towards the trunk of a tree on the other side of the road, and slammed Mary into the pinewood. Maeve flew off the spear and skidded on her stomach into the woods.

Maeve stood up and brushed off. The lack of a functioning nervous system had impaired her pain receptors-- an advantage of being undead.

Maeve walked toward Mary. The ghostly legend was hunched over, immobile. Her torso was pierced all the way through. Maeve was satisfied that she had summarily defeated the poltergeist within the remains of a seemingly innocent woman, named Mary.

Maeve began the slow walk to St. James, but Bud's car began to spin on its roof. She saw Mary's head was raised from the slumped position. She shook it. The car careened and struck Maeve square in the chest. She lay motionless while Mary's form began to wither into bones and dust. Maeve couldn't move as she watched the poltergeist leave the remains of Mary.

23

GHOSTLY GUARDIANS

Bert reached the long gravel driveway that led to St. James Church and the cemetery therein. Nothing appeared to be out of place until he reached the gateway. The gravestones to the left of the church were randomly placed and weathered in disrepair, crooked and cracked. The wrought iron bars of the gate were bent as he approached the limestone-stained exterior of the church building. He entered the Church through the front doors which faced away from Archer Avenue and looked around for a member of the Order of St. Michael.

"Hello? Anyone present?" Bert searched around with his advanced optics for any signs of life. Nothing.

He examined the large wooden cross hanging over the altar and then tried to move closer to examine a golden-trimmed box. Some kind of force prevented him from going further. His optics could not see any physical barrier. Ever stubborn, Bert continued pushing, but this time the force shoved back and almost knocked him off the altar.

"What the hell is limiting my progress?"

As if in reply, a form took shape by the box. It looked like a young, pale man wearing suspenders and holding a pick ax. Next to the ghostly apparition, another taller man with broad shoulders appeared holding a piece of jagged limestone. His face looked older than the first and weathered from hard work. They both floated in front of the golden box behind the altar.

"Oh dear, oh dear." The voice came from behind Bert.

He turned around and saw an older man with a bald head. He wore robes down past his ankles.

"It's okay Flannery boys. I can take it from here. This boy seems harmless," the older man said. The two ghosts disappeared from the altar.

"I presume you are a monk of the Order," Bert said facing the older man.

"Father Martinez, and yes, I am the monk assigned to this parish. One can only assume you are here because of the poltergeist that afflicted and disturbed the remains of Mary Sobieksi. Where is Maeve? I did page her correctly, didn't I?"

"Yes, we received your summons. Maeve is currently battling said poltergeist now further down Archer. Who were those ghosts on the altar?"

"Those were the Flannery boys. Two Irish brothers who died building the I and M canal a long, long, time ago. They are guardian angels. I only call up them in times of great duress, which has been happening more and more frequently, sadly. I have been sealing the tree in the area every night per my duty. Yet, still there is much evil paranormal activity like, for instance, this poltergeist. Are you sure Maeve can handle this poltergeist? I tried sealing it with the power of the sacred tree but it broke away from my power. I was hoping the power of multiple monks would be able to contain it." Father Martinez sat in the pew in front of Bert. His breath was labored.

"Maeve has unique abilities. I am sure she will be up to the battle..." Bert's internal warning system sounded. Maeve triggered the alarm as Bert pinpointed the alarm with his internal GPS. "...I am afraid we must go to the aid of Maeve now!"

"We can take my car," Father Martinez said, standing up from the pew.

"I can get us there faster. Climb on my back." Bert turned around and crouched.

"A piggy-back ride...I am too old for such nonsense."

Bert turned his head. "Trust me. We must hurry."

Father Martinez hopped on and Bert held the monk's legs.

"Tighten your grip. I won't feel it. I am a synthetic android. Be not afraid."

Bert began a brisk walk out of the church with Father Martinez on his back then gradually increased his speed.

"Hold on." Bert moved faster and faster. By the time he hit Archer Avenue, he was moving the speed limit of 45 mph.

"AH! HAHAHAHAHAHA!" The good priest yelled and laughed as Bert took him on a thrill ride. Bert began to slow upon seeing Bud's totaled car and Maeve laying on the side of the road. Father Martinez hopped off his back, collected himself, then ran to Maeve. He knelt down next to her.

"Oh no my dear. En el nombre del Padre, y del Hilo, y del Espirtu Santo..."

Bert scanned Maeve's injuries then called Bud.

"We have an emergency situation. The poltergeist is still at large and Maeve is badly injured. Severe chest contusions. Head trauma. She still has some fine motor skills as she was able to trigger the silent alarm I connected to her cross. How is the investigation going?"

Bud's voice burst from the receiver. "Bert! The investigation is of no matter. This is not a casual conversation. A friend is in need. Her body can only take so much. She will be beyond repair if we don't restart her heart. Teleport her to the Tower. Then transfer all the equipment. The final pieces were delivered via a rush order to the house this morning. Let's move now. There are storms coming. We are fortunate. Time for the Frankenstein Protocol."

24

SEARS TOWER OF TERROR

"Have you gathered all the samples you need of this so-called elixir?" Bud walked over to Ivy who was putting more shavings into a plastic bag. She was on her fifth bag.

"Almost done. I did tell you it would take some time. Okay, we can go." Ivy sealed the last plastic bag.

"We shall teleport out of here to my original spot on campus near the Museum of Science and Industry. I must make haste." Bud stood next to Ivy, who held all her samples.

"Wait will these be intact with teleportation?" Ivy asked.

"Yes, of course. Don't drop them." Bud readied the app on his phone to trigger teleportation. "Anything else you need?"

Ivy and Bud looked around one more time at the dimly lit, old laboratory where the atomic bomb had been developed.

"Wait." Ivy pulled the string of the singular light bulb hanging from the ceiling.

"Here we go." Bud triggered teleportation.

The early morning light was dim. Storm clouds gathered. Ivy reeled from the experience of suddenly shifting from one spot in three-dimensional space to another. She dropped the bags, knelt down and felt the grass on a field in front of the Museum as a comforting reminder of reality.

"When you have recovered, I would suggest furthering your study of these samples. Also, I would suggest staking out the Institute. It is unclear if the gallery will still be closed today or just the offices upstairs. Needless to say we should watch for any suspicious people entering or exiting the building."

"Bud, I know I have been difficult but I hope your friend is okay. I hope you can help her because I could have helped Trish and I didn't. I was too scared." Ivy looked down. Her bottom lip quivered.

"It is highly likely that you would not be standing here if you entered the fray. You notified the police and that was the right thing to do, Ivy. We will catch her killer. We have solid leads. Tally ho."

Bud found himself reeling from a gust of wind atop the tubular-constructed icon, the Sears Tower, now known as the Willis Tower. Once the world's tallest building, the view from the top was incredible. Bud was not afraid of heights, but one could not help but be intimidated by this extreme. The cars below were ant-like. The massive white antennae next to Bud acted as the ant queen. The Tower commanded Chicago's skyline.

Bert was setting up Maeve's medical bed. The storm clouds rolled in from the west and covered Chicagoland. Around the medical bed were dynamos ready to collect electricity and channel it into Maeve's undead body through a series of ports that were strategically placed near her major arteries and heart. A helmet would be used to stimulate and remind Maeve's brain to signal a heartbeat. Signals from the heart to the brain and from the brain to the heart were needed to stimulate human life.

"The deep brain stimulation electrodes are ready in that helmet Bert?"

"Yes, sir they should implant with no problem as it has already been tested on Parkinson's patients."

"I know they work, Bert. I just wanted to know if they were ready."

"I assembled them myself," Bert answered.

"That is why I asked Bert. You are the one who assembled them."

Bud examined Maeve who lay on the medical bed as Bert bounced around setting everything up. Her skull was exposed and cracked in the back of her head. Her chest was severely bruised when Mary hit her with Bud's car. These new injuries added to her already bruised back from the Capone battle.

Her vocal apparatus still worked, "What are you going to do to me, Bud?"

"We are going to employ the same principles outlined in the Diary of Victor Frankenstein to stimulate your brain and heart."

"You are going to electrocute me?" Maeve said.

"In a way yes. A very controlled amount of electricity will flow through your body. Be not afflicted with anxiety, dear Maeve."

"This isn't the way. What happened to me is of a supernatural origin Bud. Practical medicine won't reverse this."

Maeve struggled to sit up while Bud applied butterfly stitches to open wounds and wrapped her torso and the back of her head with medical wrappings. She was weak.

"Nonsense Maeve. If I invented a working teleportation system, I most confidently and stridently can reverse undeath."

The first raindrops hit Bud's forehead. The wind kicked up. Clouds shielded their view to the city below.

"Bud, don't do this," Maeve pleaded.

"This will work." Bud lay her down on the medical bed.

Thunder rumbled. The sound traveled from west to east and grew louder and louder.

"Bert, it is time. Plug everything in to that access panel. Get the laptop up and running. I will monitor the current. We will pull from the Tower's internal electric power then generate the rest from the lightning strikes. Once we channel the power from the building into the equipment and then to the antennae, we should attract some lighting strikes."

BOOM! CRACK! A lightning strike sounded from a couple miles away.

The rain pelted Bud and Bert. Bud wiped the rain from his eyebrows. Bert slipped but secured the laptop into a protective shell and handed it to Bud.

Bud sat on the roof. Puddles formed in different spots around him. Bud adjusted the dynamos and made sure Maeve's DBS helmet was secure over her head.

"Step away Bert. In fact, perhaps you should go as you don't want to get struck by lightning."

"It appears I can't teleport out of here, sir, with the storm interference."

"Okay then step away. I am about to boot everything up."

"Bad idea." Maeve said.

BOOM! CRACK! BOOM!

Bud started the laptop and secured the power from the Tower into the dynamos and equipment. He pulled so much power from the Tower it started to vibrate. Bud and Bert slid sideways. The mighty wind was causing the top of the Sears Tower to sway.

"Oh shit!" Bud exclaimed.

They only slid a few feet before sliding back. The rain pelted them.

CRACK!

The lightning bolts increased. One hit one of the large, white antenna, the power traveled down to the dynamos surrounding Maeve. The foot end of the medical bed moved with the sway but it's weight kept her stable.

Bud wiped his brow and checked the levels of the laptop then tried to initiate and control the flow of the electrical current into Maeve. He failed to register a heartbeat.

The sway caused Bud and Bert to slide again. This time a dynamo fell over and rolled away from Maeve's medical bed. It was still connected to power from the Tower. Bud lay in a puddle in front of the rolling dynamo that sparked its way toward him. Bert jumped in front of the dynamo and caught it. The electrical current enveloped and jolted Bert. Bud could smell the synthetic skin melting.

His android assistant had saved him.

25

BEDKNOBS NO BROOMSTICKS

Bert vibrated and flailed. His voice apparatus buzzed loudly. The sound of Bert's suffering sickened Bud. Even though Bert was just a robot. Bud still cared. He did not know how much more Bert could take. The current that was supposed to revive Maeve was now destroying Bert.

Bud pulled his leather jacket over his head and walked, preferring not to run and slip, to the generator. Another lightning strike coursed through the antennae and sparked the dynamos around Maeve. She was still safe as Bud was not able to activate the helmet or the ports connected to her.

The rain dwindled for a moment and Bud was able to unplug the equipment from the electrical generator underneath the antennae. He looked towards Bert who still couldn't pull away from the dynamo. The current from the antenna was too strong. Suddenly, Bert was able to throw the dynamo off of himself but did so with such incredible force that it flew off the side of the building. The bed was attached to the dynamo. Maeve's bed rolled away from the spot in front of the antennae and towards the eastern section of the roof.

"Oh dear!"

Bud ran to grab Maeve. His heart beat rapidly. His disbelief was suspended by imminent doom. The bed rolled closer and closer to the edge of the rooftop. Maeve attempted to scoot off the foot of the bed but was too weak.

"I've got you! I've got you!" Bud jumped towards the bed, reaching for Maeve's foot. The head of bed tipped over the edge. Bud's leap seemed to last forever. His fingertips touched the tip of her shoe, but he ultimately failed and fell on his hands.

The middle of the bed tipped over the edge if it went any further Maeve would have to submit to the power of gravity.

Bud popped back up. He leaned over the edge and secured Maeve's ankle with one hand and pulled back on the bed to hold it in place with the other. Bud's lack of strength was temporarily rendered irrelevant due to the adrenaline pumping through his veins in a stream as mighty as the torrential rain.

"Maeve I am going to need to you to disconnect yourself. The wires in the ports need to be disconnected or you will go down with the ship as it were." Bud's grip was still strong.

Maeve was angled, not quite upside down, but close to it.

She pushed off the helmet.

"Don't drop me, Bud."

Bud could only grimace.

She removed the plugs from her chest, then her arms, but couldn't reach her legs. A sit up from a nearly upside down position would prove difficult, given her weakened state.

Another dynamo connected to the bed blew off the roof which made the weight pulling against Bud greater.

His grip weakened.

Maeve's arms reached for the plugs near her femoral arteries. She leaned up with all her might, but fell back.

"One more... time... you can... can do it, my dear," Bud urged.

BOOM. More thunder rolled.

Maeve reached up and unplugged both of her legs with one fell swoop.

Bud loosed his grip on the bed. The bed and dynamos crashed down the carbon-tinted tubular structure towards the ground. It skated off the sides of the building. Glass shattered and sprayed out into wind.

Bud used both hands to pull Maeve up to the roof. The thunderstorm rolled toward the lake to the east. The rain remained steady. Maeve and Bud laid next to each other exhausted.

"Um, where's Bert? Couldn't he have helped you?" Maeve asked.

"I am afraid he may be incapacitated."

Bert appeared. He is face had been burnt off. The cold metal of his skeletal face remained. His optics were huge and terrifying to look at. He buzzed and sparked.

"Bert...you...still operational?" Bud asked as he sat up.

Bert let out a low, guttural growl then jumped off the top of the Tower.

26

SINKHOLES AND SURPRISES

"Bert!" Bud lifted himself off the ground and ran to the edge Bert had jumped off. The clouds still blocked his vision to the ground. He heard Bert hit the ground. The sound was not unlike an artillery cannon. Bud's heart dropped. His grand plan to revive Maeve had failed and led to disastrous consequences.

"Don't you think you ought to get down there." Maeve was still on her back.

She raised herself up on her elbows. "Let's hope he didn't kill anyone."

"It is still a bit early for the heaviest throes of rush hour. I am sure Bert survived the fall. What is most worrisome is why he jumped off one of the tallest buildings in the world? With the storm past our current vector, I should be able to check his programming with the mobile."

Bud reached for his phone and found himself surprised it was still in his jacket pocket. A diagram of Bert's body showed on Bud's screen. Bert's body flashed red. Emergency mode.

"This is most unfortunate. Bert is in an elevated emergency mode which means all his processing resources are being spent on physicality. He is basically as strong as Frankenstein's original monster. With the damage from the storm, who knows what damage he can wreak. He will possibly perceive everything as a threat." Bud grabbed the wet hair on the top of his head.

"Well, can't you just shut him down?" Maeve said.

Bud attempted to hack into Bert with his mobile. Nothing.

"I am afraid the damage from the storm has severed my direct connection with his operating system. I can monitor him but not control him."

"Bud, get down there. Now. Shut him down. Then get up here and help me. I told you your experiment wouldn't work." She laid back down on the rooftop. Her strength was sapped. The rain turned to a drizzle.

"I shall return." Bud teleported to a destination marker he had left near Union Station months ago. The station was only a couple blocks from Willis Tower. The first flood of workers emerged from the station on their daily march to work. Bud joined the crowd but pushed his way through, faster than even the most impatient walkers.

Sirens blared.

"Shit. Shit. Bert, don't let the sound of first responder vehicles lead me to you!"

People largely ignored Bud's outburst.

A block away from the Willis Tower, Bud searched for a sign of Bert. The Fire Department roared to the front of the building. An ambulance and then the CPD, made their way to what Bud surmised was a significant hole in the ground. Bud ran past the yellow tape to a group of firemen looking into the hole.

"Yeah, gotta be a sinkhole or somethin,'" a fireman said.

"This'll be a nightmare right at frick'n rush hour. And I was almost done with my damn shift," another fireman said.

"Esteemed gentlemen of the Chicago Fire Department, I would suggest you move away from the hole in the ground. I am afraid it is not a natural sinkhole as that would be highly improbable given the nature of this street." Bud stood next to them.

"Who da hell are you?" the fireman next to Bud said.

"It is advisable that we all step away from this fabricated, not-at-all naturally occurring sinkhole," Bud said.

The same low growl Bert let out before jumping, sounded from the hole. It got louder and louder.

Bert flew out of the hole and rose at least twenty feet in the air. Debris from the street sprayed out behind him and pelted Bud and the firemen.

"What da hell is dat?!" a fireman yelled.

"That, my dear civil servant is the cause of the hole in the ground."

Bert landed on the hood of a cop car. The back of the car sprung up as the hood crumpled underneath Bert's weight. The cops inside the vehicle were in shock. Their eyes wide. They froze. A monster had smashed their engine.

Bud Hutchins, the genius-inventor, witnessed his creation nearly kill someone.

Bert stepped off the hood and onto the street. He surveyed his surroundings. Bud could tell the android viewed all the emergency responders as threats.

Another two cops emerged from their squad cars. Their guns were pointed at Bert, "Get down on your knees now."

He turned to the cops, the skin torn from his face, and his optics bulged unnaturally.

Bud had to break one of his rules. He had to lure Bert away from the cops.

He needed a gun.

27

RAMPAGE

Bud had only a few seconds before Bert would react to the guns the cops wielded and pointed. Bert's emergency code prompted him to respond with extreme prejudice at any gun aimed at him or Bud.

Bud surveilled the situation. Bert's left leg sparked. It must have been damaged in his leap off the Willis Tower, and this would surely slow him. Bud still assessed only risk, but a risk worth taking. Bert acted as the perfect distraction. Bud positioned himself behind one of the police officers and watched as Bert began to limp towards the officers with intent to destroy their weapons.

"You can shackle me later!" Bud tackled one of the officers from behind. The young officer fell to the ground. The grip of his revolver hit the pavement hard and bounced out of his hands. Bert turned away from the cop on the ground. The other police officer shot at Bert, but the bullet bounced off his head, leaving a burn mark on his steel skull.

The cop who had fired his sidearm cowered. Bert overcame the officer. The crunching of the cop's right hand terrified Bud. Bert crushed bones and metal.

Bud grabbed the loose gun from the ground.

"Bert!" Bud pointed the gun.

The dysfunctional android turned to Bud. The cop knelt and screamed from pain as Bert loosed his grip. Bud waved the gun in front of Bert, egging him on. Bud knew Bert's optics tracked the gun.

Bud began to run east on Adams towards Michigan Avenue. He hoped to help Bert jump in the lake away from the city center. Bert limped but limped faster than any human ever could. He was only a couple feet behind Bud's fastest speed.

Bud ran down the middle of Adams, which was a one-way street where traffic moved west. Bert and Bud ran east. Bud kept to middle of the street, hoping that the oncoming traffic would slow his android assistant down as Bert would have to dodge the cars.

Bert didn't dodge. Bert crushed a Mercedes' hood. Then sideswiped a black SUV with his shoulder sending it into a side of a building. The rest of the oncoming traffic braked. A cab rear-ended a small economy car and the frame jolted off the road and hit a hydrant. Water sprayed everywhere.

Bud heard the sounds of twisted, heavy metal and turned around. Still in the center of the street, the cars around Bud had stopped and watched the devastation Bert wrought on rush hour.

"Shit. Shit. Shit. Egregious, excessive mayhem is not in your code Bert!" Bud backtracked toward the dysfunctional droid. Bert's head spun around in circles. He likely was waiting for another car to drive towards him, so he could destroy it.

Bud walked towards Bert. He hoped that perhaps Bert would finally stop his rampage. Maybe the traffic worked in Bud's favor after all.

"Bert, it is I, Bud Hutchins, your creator." The robot's head still spun in circles.

"Bert, if your audio nodules are still operational. I need you to stand down. I am going to lay the firearm down on the ground. There is no need for emergency mode anymore. We are safe." Bud put the revolver on the ground and moved toward Bert, hoping to get close enough to teleport him back home.

Bert's head still rotated like a bad special effect from an iconic 70s horror film.

Bud was two feet away from Bert. A voice from behind yelled, "Freeze!" Another officer pointed a gun at Bud's back. Bert's head stopped rotating. His optics honed in on the officer's gun.

"Put away the gun now, officer. Clearly this is no ordinary perpetrator. As you can see from the devastation around us and the fact that he has no face should indicate the sensitivity of our current quagmire." Bud kept still but his eyes widened.

Bert moved forward and threw Bud onto the sidewalk. Bud landed on his right elbow, but quickly looked towards the street. The police officer was running away with Bert in hot pursuit.

"Good chap." Bud rubbed his elbow then ran back into the street. Bud saw Bert chase the cop toward Michigan Avenue. Bud picked the revolver back up and ran as fast he could while supporting his injured elbow.

The cop and Bert turned left onto Michigan Avenue. Bud had almost reached Michigan when he heard the feint sound of Ravel's "Bolero" coming from Orchestra Hall. The melodious song was rudely interrupted by three loud gunshots.

28

LION HEAD

Bud turned the corner and onto the ever-busy Michigan Avenue, the world famous street was buzzing as usual with traffic and pedestrians. He noticed Bert rampaging into the lobby of Orchestra Hall, home to the renowned Chicago Symphony Orchestra. Bud rubbed his elbow and sped up to close the gap between him, Bert and the cop, who heeded his advice and ran. Bud didn't think it wise to lead Bert into a rehearsal of the CSO. Alas, here he was.

Bud paused for a moment outside the bronze doors that stood between him and mayhem. He took a breath and barreled into the ticket box office area of Orchestra Hall.

Bert was scanning the room. His artificial skin was now peeling off his neck and his optics looked cold and mechanical. Three bullets had left burn markings on Bert's torso.

The rising, almost deafening, chords of "Bolero" pulsed from the concert hall into the box office. The cop must have jumped through one of the ticket windows. He was hiding behind the counter.

Bud was surprised Bert hadn't picked up on the obvious whereabouts of the officer, but the robot was severely damaged, it is likely that the only scan his optics would pick up would be a gun.

"Bert! You blithering idiot! It is I, Bud Hutchins, your creator. I command you to cease this needless subroutine. There is no emergency. You are the sole cause of current events."

Bert turned his head.

Bud hoped his commands would somehow be obeyed by the destructive android.

They stared each other down. Bud's heart pounded. He hid the revolver behind his back.

Bert took a step.

The music reached its fevered crescendo. The brilliant horn section blasted the rhythmic, repetitive, notes. Bert turned towards the loud music and ran towards the doors of the concert hall.

"Oh no, you bloody don't!" Bud readied the revolver. His reluctance to shoot was vanquished by his monstrous creation's seemingly unending path of devastation.

He pulled the trigger. The bullet bounced off the back of Bert's head. Bert was smashing one of the doors leading into the hall when he felt the ping. He spun towards Bud.

"That's it old chap! Follow me!" Bud ran out of Orchestra Hall and back onto Michigan Avenue.

Bert busted through the bronze doors of Orchestra Hall, leaving them in a contorted mess. Bud weaved across Michigan Avenue between vehicles stopped by the numerous traffic lights that peppered the famous street. He ran towards one of the original buildings of the Columbian Exposition of 1893, the Art Institute. Bud jumped multiple steps of the grand stone staircase at a time. Bert followed. He'd surprisingly left the cars stopped in traffic alone, but sadly did not spare one of the famous lions that adorned the entrance of the art museum.

Bud thought the Art Institute would be open. He had pulled and pushed the doors. He even had used the butt of the revolver to crack a door. Nothing worked. Defeated, he turned to face his creation. One of the signature Bronze lion's heads roared through the air toward him. Bud dropped to the pavement. The lion's head smashed through the glass doors granting Bud the entry he had desired.

"Most appropriate." Bud gingerly stepped over the proud lion's head and into the foyer.

The alarm blared. A lone security guard rushed to call for help behind the admissions desk.

"Hey! You can't be in here!" The guard yelled.

"Believe me, my presence is not voluntary. Where might I ask is the Medieval Hall of Armor?"

"What the?" He saw the deranged Bert coming up the stairs. "Um, straight ahead and to the right."

"Thank you and you might want to hide behind the admissions counter."

Bert stomped towards Bud.

The guard quickly ducked.

Bert kept on towards Bud.

The white walls of the Institute showcased various galleries of Impressionist and Classical art. Bert left the walls untouched. He had already left his own impression upon the Institute with the lion's head redecoration.

Bud reached the end of the Hall and turned right. Ahead lay the Hall of Armor--the detailed, vast, collection of medieval weaponry and knightly garments. Bullets were not working with Bert but perhaps other weapons would. Bud recalled the weapon collection in Beauregard and hoped Maeve was okay still on the top of the Willis Tower.

Bullets didn't work on the android, but they did work on glass. Bud shot three through a display case. The mechanized stomping of a severely damaged Bert was getting louder and louder. Bud had little time to prepare.

29

MEDIEVAL TIME

Bud's vision was limited yet sufficient. The knight's helmet was heavy. The face guard jutted outwards and he struggled to keep his head from drooping forward. His elbow hurt like hell. He stood to the left of the entrance to Hall of Armor. The metal gauntlets felt tight and very cold. The sword's weight intimidated him, yet he had to find the strength to wield it. He hid behind a full-size knight mannequin. He hoped the pain in his elbow wouldn't weaken his swing or aim too much. He need to strike Bert with a fatal blow.

The wiring in Bert's neck from the main CPU in his head to the power cell in his chest was the android's only structural weakness. Bud gripped the hilt of broadsword as Bert stomped closer and closer to the entrance of the Hall.

The alarm bells rang with a deafening sonic assault and soon more of Chicago's finest would be searching the building. Bert's rampage had to end now.

Bud laid the gun on the ground in front of the display case where he hid. The trap was set.

Bert entered the room.

Bud was just to the right of Bert behind the knight. He saw his creepy optics scan the room.

Bert's head lowered. Bert bent to destroy the gun.

Bud pushed the knight mannequin onto Bert. The clanking of metal on metal pinged louder than the alarms. Bert lay prone under the heavy armor only for a few seconds. He quickly pushed off the armor and struggled to his knees.

Bud raised the broadsword and aimed at Bert's neck. Bud's elbow throbbed as he used all his might to bring the heavy blade down on Bert. The blade stopped abruptly when it sunk into Bert's neck. The robot fell to the ground and spastically shook as he lay prone once again. He attempted to grab the sword. Bud let the hilt go and looked at the medieval weapon embedded in his friend's neck.

Shouts and footfalls down the hall announced the arrival of the cops.

"Sorry to do this Bert!" Bud kicked down on the sword to finish the sever.

Sparks flew. One more kick would do it. SNAP.

"Freeze kid!" Eight police officers reached the Hall of Armor.

Bud picked up Bert's severed head.

"It is not as it seems. Gentlemen, my apologies."

Bud, with Bert's head cradled in his arms, disappeared.

30

VIOLATED

Someone had been here. They had tried to cover their tracks but had left too much out of place. The microscope had been moved at least two inches. The samples had been tampered with. The book had been picked up and put down in the wrong place.

He couldn't bear to see his research stolen from him, when he was so close. He had to be the first. Lab rats would take too long. No clinical trials.

Now is the time.

The Elixir's missing ingredient had been found.

Who else would be on to him? Who was down here?

Now is the time.

He grabbed a beaker. The proper application of heat should finalize the mix. Then he would consume it and show the world.

The Bunsen burner filled the air with the pungent smell of natural gas. The singular lightbulb swayed from his rapid movements, creating a chaotic atmosphere--one of madness and aggression.

He took shavings from each of the ancient artifacts put them in a mixing bowl. He added water. The brittle shavings dissolved quickly in his mixture. He poured the chunky, thick mix into the beaker that rested on a small dish over the burner. The heat would purify it. His eyes grew wide. A puff of green smoke billowed from the glass beaker.

He could barely contain himself. He lived for the elation of discovery, his mood joyous when fortune smiled upon him, yet dour with misfortune. Dangerously so.

Once the smoke dissipated, he picked up the hot beaker with his bare hands. Never mind the pain. He opened his mouth. His heart pounded with anticipation. He drank.

The burning tore through his esophagus, to the lining of his stomach. His heart rate spiked. He grabbed his chest, certain he would not recover this time. He fell to his knees.

His crouched and smacked the ground with an open palm. He lay on his stomach panting like a rabid dog. Foam bubbled from his mouth.

31

HUBRIS

Bud dropped Bert's head on the desk in the computer room. He pulled the knight's helmet off. He quickly attached an intact dangling USB cord hanging from the many wires protruding from Bert's severed neck, and attached it to the desktop computer. It would take quite a while for Bert to recover, should he recover at all. Bud had little time to waste. He had left Maeve on top of one of the world's tallest buildings. He looked on his phone for the marker he used to teleport directly to the Tower. Its beacon did not show on the screen. It must have been damaged in the storm like everything and everyone else.

Bud initiated teleportation back to Union station.

The latter hours of the morning rush filled the station with slackers rushing to work.

His phone buzzed. It was Ivy. "How's your friend, Bud? She okay?"

"I am afraid she is still in a state unsuitable for sustained life. I am on my way back to her now."

"I am so sorry...I see that you had quite the tussle downtown during the middle of rush hour. Way to attract attention to yourself there, Hutchins," Ivy said.

"Oh dear, I was afraid that might happen, considering Chicago is one of the most surveilled cities in America. I've quite the mess to clean up."

"So who was the super-villain you were fighting and being thrown around by?" Ivy asked.

"That is Bert, my robotic companion. He may have suffered some damage to his mainframe..."

"What did you do to him?"

"It would have worked had the weather cooperated," Bud said.

"You can tell me all about it later. The Institute's gallery will be closed but they sent me an email since I am a volunteer, saying the building will be open for staff in the morning. I will begin my stakeout then. The artifacts I found have quite an interesting connection. I will share it with you later." Ivy hung up on him.

Bud hoped the way would be clear now that he was a minor celebrity. The local news stations kept Bert's rampage on a continuous loop. Some of the graphics on the screen said, "Terminator. Real?". They did focus more on Bert than himself which would be to his advantage.

He reached the street and saw police and emergency vehicles were still surrounding the crevice Bert had created with his ill-advised leap.

Bud could easily blend in with the 25,000 people who entered the Willis Tower on a daily basis. He joined the flow of workers filing into the lobby of the tower. He didn't realize he still wore the metal gauntlets from the Art Institute. The metal detectors at the security checkpoint lay ahead. Bud hastily removed the gauntlets from his hand and dropped them on the floor. Two women and one rather large fellow tripped on them.

"Shit! You okay? What the hell are these?" The man yelled.

Bud blended in with the rest of the crowd, creating distance between the medieval mess he made. He kept walking to the checkpoint. He followed a woman wearing a Skydeck badge. The Skydeck is the main tourist attraction of the tower and the elevator to it would bypass the other floors and get him to the 103rd floor the quickest.

Bud cleared the checkpoint, avoided the security desk, and followed the female Skydeck worker. She walked to the express tube elevator and the door opened immediately. Bud hopped in at the last second before the doors closed.

"The Skydeck doesn't open for another half hour, sir. At 9am. You shouldn't be here."

Bud looked like hell. His hair was sweaty and disheveled, sticking out in at least seven places. He held his sore elbow and he was still damp and probably smelled like sweat.

"Oh I understand that. I was called in to repair the antennas."

"You don't have any tools or anything."

"Don't need them." Bud pulled out his cellphone and waved it, "Technology these days. Just have to plug in and make some adjustments. Rough storm this morning."

Bud tried to maintain his American accent but it was so hard for him not to ease into his forced British.

The woman eased up. She had dark circles under her eyes and looked as if she suffered from a lack of sleep. She shook her head and Bud hoped she could sense no danger from him. She was much bigger than he anyway, and could summarily wipe the Skydeck with him.

The 103rd floor was impressive. The view was wonderful and much more peaceful when not having to deal with the prevailing gale-force winds.

Bud located the stairwell to the roof.

"Have a good day."

"You too." The woman was surprisingly pleasant all of a sudden.

Bud ascended the narrow staircase to the roof where Maeve lay. She was in the same exact spot he had left her. Bud wondered if the undead could suffer from paralysis. The notion's absurdity would certainly match the experiences of the day thus far.

"Oh my dear, Maeve. You okay?" Bud shook her shoulder.

"Stop shaking me." Her voice box sounded weak.

"We need to get you back to the house. It will be just a second. We can teleport out of here." Bud grabbed her under the armpits. Maeve was heavy and could barely move or give any assistance. He managed to get his arms around her torso and pushed the button on his teleportation wristband.

They arrived in the living room of his grandfather's home. Maeve became too heavy and Bud dropped her onto the carpet.

Panic built up within Bud. He shook her. She lay unconscious with her eyes wide open. Her state of being undead gave Bud no indication if Maeve, as he knew her, still existed.

"Speak. Speak!" Bud rubbed her cheek. Her big hazel eyes stared at the ceiling.

Bud feared the worst. His insistence on electrocuting her back to live state failed. She had told him it wouldn't work. Perhaps, she had been right.

Bud for the first time in his life, didn't know what to do.

A rapid knock on the front door...

Bud's eyes teared up and a single drop escaped his right eyelid and ran down his cheek. He wiped it.

The knock slowed, but was harder this time.

Bud opened the door to a short man dressed in monk's robes.

"Young man, I am Padre Martinez, a monk of the Order. I must take Maeve with me. She is no longer safe here."

32

UNCONVENTIONAL

"Whatever do you mean?" Bud asked, visibly upset.

"I was the monk of the Order who paged for assistance at St. James. The poltergeist is still at large. The violent apparition won't stop until it eliminates those with the power to stop it, the monks of the Order of St. Michael."

"Where are you to take Maeve?"

"A convent near Midway airport, formerly Lourdes High School."

"What is safe about a convent? What will the nuns do? Instill her with a powerful sense of guilt?" Bud was near hysteria.

"No nuns actually physically live there. The convent is largely empty save for a few powerful protectors."

"Do you mean ghost nuns?"

"My boy, do not mock the Lord's servants. Help me get her to the car. The convent is not far."

"How do I know you are not a nefarious foe of the Order? Show me your scar from the lash of initiation into the Order."

"Hutchins, you have little faith. You will just have to trust our Heavenly Father. Help me my boy." Father Martinez patted Bud's shoulder and looked Bud in the eyes, "She will be safe with me, Bud."

Bud sighed. He looked at Maeve. Another tear dropped down his cheek.

"Given her state, I suppose you arriving here at this time may be considered good fortune," Bud said.

Bud and Father Martinez lifted Maeve. Bud arms wrapped around her torso again and Father Martinez held her legs.

"Is she okay?" Father Martinez said, panting.

"About that I am not certain. This is a rather complex situation. She has been through much turmoil." Bud put her head and shoulders along the backseat of Father Martinez's compact car.

"I will keep her safe my boy. We monks have seen worse." Father pushed her legs into the car. Bud went around the other side of the car and pulled her to a safe position on her back.

Father Martinez drove off with Maeve in the backseat.

Bud hoped the Father could keep her safe--if there was anything left of Maeve to protect. His shoulders slumped from pressure of it all. He needed no nun to spark the guilt. He felt the full measure of his failed experiment as he watched Maeve drive away.

His phone buzzed. Bud took a deep breath. There was still work to do--a murder mystery to solve.

It was Ivy. "Hey Bud, I am on a bench outside of the Institute. I have much to share."

"I shall teleport to you shortly. There is much to..." Bud initiated teleportation.

He arrived again, in front of the Museum of Science and Industry, "...do."

"Did you just teleport while on the phone with me? Amazing," Ivy said.

"I did and it is not that impressive." Bud jogged towards the Institute.

"You are in a mood. Anyway, no suspicious characters have entered the building as of this morning. Just some volunteers and someone to open the door. Also, some of the professors did come to the building early today. They didn't look so good."

"What about the basement entry around back?"

"After you left I set up a camera there. Nothing."

Bud could see Ivy's stark black hair and glasses. She had stacks of books next to her on the bench. He was close. He slowed his jog.

"What is with all the books?" Bud asked.

"The elixir, Bud. I have been dying to tell you!"

Bud was extremely sensitive to the word dying at the moment. He grimaced.

"You really are in a bad mood. Anyway, the books are on neuroscience. It turns out the ancients were on to something. The shavings I got from the ancient artifacts in the lab? They all have one connection: they were believed to hold properties that enhance the mind."

"To what degree of enhancement?" Bud asked.

"Genius level enhancement and not just book smarts either, think charisma, leadership skills, tactical skills, inventiveness...the list goes on and on."

"Oh dear, Ivy. A drink that gives one a high intelligence quotient? What rubbish!"

"We have to get back into Tricia's office. It may very well be all rubbish, but there was a reason all of these items were gathered and connected in that lab. We have to see if there is a tie between what Trish was working on and the elixir."

33

THE PROPER APPLICATION

Ivy entered the lobby first. Since she was a regular at the Institute, she likely would not raise alarms. The volunteers were chatting about the previous night's events. They quieted down upon seeing Ivy, knowing she was close with Tricia. The Gallery would be closed today and the offices would close at noon. The staff was allowed to come into recover any work they needed to meet deadlines and class requirements.

Ivy and Bud headed up the stairs together. Bud struggled to keep pace; his exhaustion was great.

"What do you know of Tricia's research?" Bud asked.

"I know that she and Covington were working closely together on something big for the Board of Regents position that Covington wanted. She wanted to keep it under wraps, even from me. Apparently it would have been earth-shattering. That's why I think the elixir may be the key."

Ivy walked down the hall back towards Covington's office, the site where her friend was brutally murdered. There were two people in other offices working. The police tape was still on Covington's door, but it was open. Bud and Ivy ducked under and into the series of connected offices. Ivy cringed.

"Odd that the door was open. It is technically still a crime scene isn't it?" Bud observed.

"Maybe the cops thought no one would dare enter the area?" Ivy said.

"That is highly unlikely. I think someone has been here. Covington perhaps? Mourning the loss of his mistress? Here to gather his Board of Regents proposal as you said? Did you see him enter the building this morning?"

"No, I didn't see him. I did stop at the library first so he may have gotten here earlier than me. I figured your friend Bert could keep reviewing the video feeds that is until I saw him on the morning news show. Wait. Tricia was Covington's mistress? Did you say that?" Ivy stopped and stared at Bud.

"Yes, I figured she would have told you of her indiscretions. You two were friends."

"No, she didn't tell me. You don't think he killed her do you?"

"According to his wife, he was with her last night at their favorite pizza place. He was devastated upon hearing the news of Tricia's demise," Bud said.

"Did anyone call the pizza place to confirm the Covingtons were there?" Ivy asked.

Bud shook his head, slowly. Another mistake.

"That would be a good idea don't you think, Hutchins?! Mrs. Covington, your client, may be lying to you!" Ivy's face turned red.

"Why would she hire me if she knew her husband did it? Makes not a lick of sense."

"Find out what their favorite pizza place is and call them later when they open. Right now we have to see if we can find any connection to the elixir in here."

Bud scanned the area with his phone the artifacts that had been strewn on the floor were still there.

"Those are more of the same preserved artifacts that we found in the lab," Ivy said.

"What exactly are these?"

"They are dried food containers that must have trace elements of different food that are known to boost brain function: beets, greens, fish, avocado, some carbs, etc. They might not be exactly those foods but foods with similar properties, when mixed and applied properly into liquid form, the elixir is ready to consume."

"What happens if you don't mix and apply properly?"

"Well funny you should mention that because look at this?" Ivy held up a picture of cave paintings that had been circled by Tricia, Ivy noticed her handwriting in an annotation.

"What in the bloody hell does that have to do with anything?"

"You don't know?" Ivy laughed.

"No, I don't bloody know. There, you have me. What is it?"

"Cinnabar, the red paint that contains mercury. Early man used it all the time. Another ingredient is mercury, that if not properly applied could kill you. That is what happens when not properly mixed."

34

HISTORICAL IMPLICATIONS

Ivy and Bud's curious minds were feasting on their new-found revelatory details of Covington's research.

"I do remember from AP World History class, that ShiHuangDi, the emperor of China, drank mercury thinking it would grant him eternal youth." Bud examined the picture.

"Okay, I was a chemistry major before and mercury when introduced to the human brain causes some interesting reactions in neurons. If the other ingredients prepare the brain and energize the amino acids in our neurons then the proper application of mercury could act as binding agent, like a lattice reaching out to other neurons. The lattice would maximize the likelihood of multiple neurotransmitters firing all at once, which many believe is what separates the genius from the moron. Or me from you." Ivy laughed.

"Very amusing. Have you invented teleportation?" Bud scoffed.

"Or it could even mean that the elixir somehow pulls the two hemispheres of the brain closer together? Like in Einstein's brain! The interaction between the two hemispheres is also another reason for explaining genius."

Bud examined more pictures on Tricia's desk including a map of civilizations.

"It is therefore feasible, that Covington thought he could prove man's greatest achievements through the use of the elixir. He has lines crossing the map from Mesopotamia and Africa to China and Japan then to Europe back to the Middle East again to Europe and on to the Americas."

Bud turned the map over. "Look at these names Ivy." Bud showed her.

"Hammurabi, Buddha, Confucius, David, Augustus, Christ, Constantine, Muhammad, Saladin, various popes, Medici, Da Vinci, Louis, Elizabeth...it goes on and on to the Founding Fathers." Ivy grinned.

"It gives whole new meaning to the phrase, 'must be in the water'," Bud said.

"If Covington could prove the elixir is real it would change history. Wars could have been fought not over land and wealth but the elixir itself."

"This is quite intense. Perhaps, Tricia was killed because of this information. Perhaps Covington did want her dead. Wanted all the acclaim for himself? Or someone else in the office wants it and Covington is next on the hit list?"

Bud and Ivy stared at each other in amazement.

"We have to get into the gallery and see if any one comes out of that tunnel. The beaker makes me think that whoever was working down there might actually be consuming it. I did hear Tricia say something like 'you are making yourself sick' right before she was killed. She was talking to a man with a deep voice that I'd never heard before. Lord knows what effect the elixir has on people, if any. It could be dangerous. Safe to say that whoever used that lab is definitely our killer," Ivy said.

35

THE MUMMY

Bud and Ivy teleported back into the Gallery using the same marker they had used the night before. They took up a position behind the Khorsabad relief in the Mesopotamian section to observe the Ancient Egyptian area. They kept particular watch over square mummy case they knew hid a passage to a secret lab underneath Chicago Met University. The lights were off, but there were small windows along the top of the tall ceiling that provided enough light for them to see the mummy case.

Ivy monitored the back door entrance on her phone.

Bud watched the case in short bursts between using his cellphone to search pizza places near the Covington's home in Lakeview. It nagged at him that Ivy had pointed out his trust in Mrs. Covington had blinded him from the details. He also had badly needed the funds for his attempt to revive Maeve. The whole situation made his stomach churn.

"Uh, Bud are you watching the case? What are you doing?" Ivy whispered.

"I can do two things at once," Bud said, scrolling through the pizza place listings.

"Highly unlikely." Ivy stared at her phone as well.

"Just when I commence to find you mildly amusing, you say things of a cutting nature." Bud looked up from his phone. There was movement.

The movement didn't come from the case itself but from the contents within the case. The mummy in the display case unfurled its body. Glass from the case shattered and sprayed all over the floor before Bud's eyes. A blue hue similar to the one surrounding Capone emanated from the dimly lit Egyptian gallery.

"Oh dear, Father Martinez was correct. The poltergeist will stop at nothing to eliminate us." Bud took a step back and knocked into Ivy.

"Who is us? And get off of me?" Ivy pushed him away.

"I failed to mention that I am technically, a monk of the Order of St. Michael, a sect of the Roman Catholic Church tasked with suppressing supernatural beasties like the one coming this way." Bud stayed put. Maybe the poltergeist mummy wouldn't see them.

The reanimated ancient Egyptian hands gripped the side of the display case. Its fingers were thin, brittle, decayed, yet somehow nimble. The mummy pulled itself up out of the case so that the head and torso showed. Its face was an exposed skull with no features but cheekbones framed by gaping holes where its eyes and nose used to be. Wrapping still clung to its head along the sides and top. When it hopped out of the case, Bud could see it looked frail. The power of the poltergeist, however, caused it to move with the fluidity of a professional athlete. It began to run straight towards Bud and Ivy.

Bud turned around and pushed Ivy towards the wall adjacent to the relief and away from the charging mummy. They emerged from behind the relief.

Bud and Ivy expected the mummy to be in hot pursuit as they dashed out in front in front of the Assyrian King's stone memorial.

"Where'd it go?" Ivy asked.

"It seems to have stopped behind the stone relief. Perhaps it dissipated?" Bud took a step forward weighing the decision to check or not.

The top of King Sargon's relief began to move. A rumble vibrated the ground.

"Make way!"

Bud and Ivy ran away from the toppling stone wall that fell towards them. Thousands of years of history wiped away by a bloodthirsty poltergeist. The incredible booming thud rattled and broke some of the glass in the Mesopotamian gallery. Bud and Ivy created enough distance between them and the relief to shield their eyes from all the dust the three-ton wall displaced.

There was a script carved onto the back of the relief. The mummy stood right on top. It raised its arms and the glass display cases around Bud and Ivy lifted off the floor. The mummy moved its arms forward and the cases flew towards the entry doors to the gallery. It was a mangled pile of artifacts, glass, and splintered wood.

Bud quickly searched for available destination markers to teleport to a safe location, but no markers showed. He closed and reopened the app. No markers again. Bud scrambled to check the pockets of his leather jacket, but his pockets were empty.

"Well, that is most unsettling. Someone deactivated all the destination markers. We have been summarily trapped," Bud said.

"No, we haven't! The tunnel Hutchins!" Ivy smacked her forehead.

"How do you suppose we reach said tunnel? There's a monster blocking our path! I was not wrong about our state of entrapment."

"Can't you do some magic or something? You are a monk of the Order, aren't you?"

"I am afraid I am all out of tricks."

The mummy crept towards Ivy and Bud. Its arms outstretched and they rotated clockwise. Bud looked behind him at the blocked over entryway. There was no way through. The shattered glass from the piled display cases spun in the air in a deadly twister that wound its way towards the youthful flesh of Ivy and Bud.

36

DEUS EX MARTINEZ

Bud and Ivy ran as fast they could away from the tornado of razors toward the fallen relief and mummy. They had no choice but to run for the tunnel. The mummy kept control of the twister, it preferred to fell Bud and Ivy with glass shards, rather than physically stop them.

The spinning death cloud nipped at the heels of Bud and Ivy as they made the right turn towards the Egyptian gallery. The sound of rushing air and debris fueled their speed. The back of Bud's jacket began to rip into shreds. His eyes widened as he saw the back of Ivy's black hair shoot straight back as if getting sucked into the murderous twister. Ivy slowed down and would soon be overtaken. She fell to the ground

"No!" Bud moved to grab her and drag her to the tunnel entrance.

"Espiritu Santo!"

A great bright light blinded Bud. He felt like he had hit a wall and dropped to his knees. He put his sore elbow in front of his eyes and squinted over and over to see the source of his seeming salvation.

From the center of the light a silhouette formed--a monk of the Order, Father Martinez.

"Grab her my boy! I can hold this poltergeist off for now."

Bud, without hesitation, helped Ivy to her feet. She took her glasses off and rubbed her eyes. "What the hell is happening?"

"Father Martinez has aided us in our endeavors." Bud and Ivy squinted to see the monk, holding his cross high. The light shining from the cross formed a bubble shield around them.

"I can only use my power for defense. We can move together back to the entrance. I created a path through with my light shield," Father Martinez said.

The poltergeist-powered mummy pushed the glass tornado against the light shield with tremendous force. Light vs Dark clashed in an epic struggle, Father Martinez grimaced.

"This poltergeist is too strong. I don't know how much I can hold this shield up."

"You shan't have to for much longer! Behind you is a tunnel entrance. We can escape through there. Just move back a few paces."

The good monk moved the bubble shield in coordination with Ivy and Bud. They pushed the mummy's resting place to the side, revealing the tunnel entrance.

"Okay, Father. We will head down. Can you maintain the shield and descend this ladder simultaneously?"

The light shield flickered as Father Martinez's grip on his cross weakened. The spinning shards of glass pelted the light barrier and disintegrated.

"No I am afraid I cannot but I brought friends with me."

Father Martinez moved towards the tunnel ladder, while Ivy descended into the tunnel. Bud began to follow her but stopped when he saw ghostly blue-collar workers armed with pickaxes and dynamite run towards the mummy.

"AAAAAAAH!" The ghostly workers charged the mummy, which dropped its arms. The twister stopped. Father Martinez lowered his cross. The bubble shield dissipated.

"Who are they?" Bud asked.

"They are the brave souls who built the Illinois and Michigan Canal. These immigrants took the toughest and most dangerous jobs and helped build America in order to give a future for their familias, my boy."

A burly ghost threw a rock into the mummy's torso. Another canal worker swung a pick ax that met the bandaged skull. The workers surrounded the mummy.

"Now is our chance to escape down the tunnel. Let's go!" Father Martinez yelled.

37

ELIXIR OF THE ANCIENTS

Bud, Ivy, and the good Father ran the only direction they could go: down the tunnel towards the lab. Rickety electric lights lit the path.

"We will never defeat that poltergeist. We need Maeve. The ghosts will only be able to fend it off temporarily," Father Martinez, said panting.

"Has she been able to move at all since you took her to the convent?" Bud asked.

"No, it's as if she is paralyzed. She can only move her eyes to indicate she is still with us. I have never seen anything like it. Her heart doesn't beat and she doesn't breathe. Yet, she is still with us."

"How did you know how to find me?" Bud asked.

"I prayed to the Lord. He does listen and answer."

Bud shook his head, keeping two paces ahead of the Father.

"After all this you still struggle to believe Hutchins." Father Martinez stopped to catch his breath.

Ivy was up ahead and reached the lab door.

"Come on Father, we are nearly to our destination."

"Bud, in order for you to truly become a monk of the Order, you must believe." Father Martinez leaned on the tunnel wall.

"We haven't time for a lesson in theological studies Father."

"Bud! Come on! The door is open! I think there may be a way we can save Maeve!" Ivy yelled.

"Father, we must reach Ivy."

Father Martinez stared at Bud.

"My grandfather disappeared. God wouldn't do that. There you have it. Now let us make haste." Bud turned away from the Father and ran to Ivy.

Father Martinez satisfied for the moment, followed with a slow jog.

Ivy entered the lab first. The dangling light bulb buzzed. It flickered.

"Oh hell no," Ivy gasped.

"What is it?" Bud entered the lab.

"Look." Ivy pointed to the floor.

Bud saw Professor Covington face down on the floor with a mess of saliva pooled next to his open mouth.

"Who is this man?" Father Martinez asked.

"This, Father, is Professor Covington, a prime suspect in the murder of a young woman named Tricia Pazinski, who was his teaching assistant." Bud knelt and examined the unconscious faculty member.

"He is out cold." Bud stood back up to see Ivy already fiddling with the artifacts left on the table. She picked up the beaker.

"No, no, no this is all wrong. He used the burner to boil the ingredients of the elixir. That was a mistake, obviously. Heating it may have caused dangerous chemical reactions due to the mercury in it and poisoned him."

"How can you revive Maeve, Ivy? Certainly not with this elixir? It has knocked the Professor out cold," Bud said.

"I think if I can use the formula he has here I think we should be okay. We just have to let it the formula settle... at a much cooler temperature. Yes, why not. That should work. I mean we can try."

Ivy plopped thin shavings from the ancient artifacts into the beaker. Then she picked up a clear container with a viscous silvery substance in it. Mercury. She dripped a bit into the beaker, then used her thumb to plug the hole and shake it. The contents of the beaker began to bubble.

"Try giving this to Maeve and see what happens." Ivy handed Bud the beaker.

A thundering crash filled the walls of the tunnel.

"We haven't much time. I am afraid there is only so much my ghostly protectors can do away from St James cemetery. Their source of power comes from the

Church there and we are too far away for them to maintain their strength for long. The poltergeist will soon be upon us. If that elixir will revive Maeve that will make our odds of defeating our enemy much better," Father Martinez said.

Bud grabbed the elixir from Ivy, "Might as well try it. We all must go."

"No I will stay here and gather all of his research. The poltergeist is after the two of you anyway. Just close the lab door. This material is far too sensitive to just leave here! I will be fine. Just go," Ivy insisted.

"What will you do if Covington comes to?" Bud asked.

Another crash. This time it was closer.

"I will tie him up and when the coast is clear I will call the cops to get him. Now go! Save Maeve!"

"Be safe, Ivy. I don't need another Maeve situation to occur."

"I will be safe. The elixir can possibly save your friend which is more than I could say for Tricia."

Bud nodded at Ivy. He and Father Martinez exited the lab and shut the door behind them. In the direction of the Institute, the tunnel was filled with the ongoing battle between three more canal workers and the mummy. The mummy kicked one through one of the tunnel walls. No damage was left. The worker just disappeared. The last two canal workers lifted their pickaxes and swung wildly. The mummy ducked under their wild swings and punched through both of them. They were gone in a puff of ectoplasm.

Bud and Father Martinez made sure the poltergeist saw them and began to run in the opposite direction.

"Is there a way out, Bud?"

"If the rumors are true there should be an exit that will lead us up to a soccer field on the Midway Plaisance. So yes, in theory, there is a way."

The mummy's athletic prowess was on full display as it ran towards them on its hands and feet. It seemed to double its speed and closed the gap between it and the middle-aged monk and Bud.

38

MONSTERS OF THE MIDWAY

Somehow adrenaline had kept Bud Hutchins alive and well despite how arduous the last two days have been. He and Father Martinez saw a metal ladder hanging down in the middle of the tunnel.

"That must be the way out!" Bud yelled.

The mummy galloped towards them. They both knew that climbing the ladder would most certainly slow them down enough for the mummy to catch up. They had no choice but to risk it.

"When we get to the ladder, my boy. Let me up first. I will use the power of the Holy Spirit."

Bud reached the ladder first and held the side of it while Father Martinez hurried up the ladder. There was no indication of a hatch or way out.

The mummy bounded towards them. It was only twenty feet away.

The monk stopped his climb and pulled out his wooden cross.

Fifteen feet.

Bud looked up at the Father. Everything seemed to be moving in slow motion.

Ten feet.

"Espiritu Santo!"

The mummy was five feet away.

The light pulsed again from Father Martinez's cross.

The mummy cowered.

"Come up here Hutchins! Find the hatch out of here!" Father Martinez yelled.

Bud ascended the ladder. Father Martinez moved so that one arm and leg were secured to the ladder. Bud pushed the top of the tunnel with his elbow then his head. He held the elixir in his hand. He pushed again, harder this time. Daylight poured into the tunnel.

"Let's go!" Bud climbed through the hole. Father Martinez held his cross and followed suit.

They emerged onto a turf soccer field on the Midway Plaisance, the site of the Chicago World's Fair of 1893.

"I was indeed correct!" Bud said.

"Look out Hutchins!" Father Martinez, yelled as a soccer ball hit Bud in the face.

Bud fell on his ass but managed to not spill the elixir. The women's soccer team ran over, astounded that two men had sprung up in the middle of their practice field.

"Are you okay?" One of the soccer players asked.

Bud's face turned bright red. "Nothing my rather large head can't handle."

"You don't have a big...well, I guess you sorta do." The soccer player laughed.

"Hahahaha, shake it off. There is still a poltergeist on our tail." Father Martinez helped him up.

The mummy hands reached the opening. One of the soccer players stood shocked as a dead Ancient Egyptian climbed out. Its wrappings and body still intact.

Father Martinez's compact car rumbled onto the field. The soccer team scattered. The car drove through the goal. The net stretched then gave way.

BOOM. CRACK.

The mummy burst into a cloud of dust and frail bones. Father Martinez's car made short work of the poltergeist's frail mummified form.

Bud's jaw dropped. "Who is driving the car?"

The car pulled up to them. Its doors popped open automatically.

"Oh, that would be Andriej. A Polish canal worker."

"He often prefers to stay invisible." Father Martinez entered the car.

"Right." Bud entered the backseat then secured the elixir with both hands.

Ivy gathered all she could of Covington's research. She needed something to carry it. She looked around for a bag like Covington's briefcase. She didn't find a briefcase but she did notice something she would not soon forget. The description of the footage Bud's android friend had relayed to them in the archives. Underneath the lab table was a black hoodie and black jeans. The clothes of the killer! Whatever doubt she had that Covington was responsible for the death of her friend was washed away.

She grabbed the hoodie, opened it up and began piling the books, papers, artifacts into it.

"What are you doing with my things? Give me my hoodie. I can't wear his clothes. I can't stand him. I hate him!"

Covington stood behind Ivy. His hot breath hit the back of her neck. She froze.

"Why must you steal from me like he did?!" He grabbed Ivy's shoulders and spun her around. He towered over her. His face was hairy in places it should not have been. His eyes were bloodshot, his bottom lip was large and drool seeped from it.

"I am not like him. I want to help you."

"Mr. Hyde needs no help from the likes of you."

39

HYDE IN HYDE PARK

Ivy tried to maintain her cool and think. Covington's deranged split personality, Hyde, squeezed her arms with an iron grip.

"Let me show you a way to overcome Covington." Ivy took a risk but perhaps this brutish alter-ego would listen to reason no matter how deranged he was.

"I can show you a way to use the elixir to permanently rid yourself of Covington, so that only you will remain and never have to fight him off again."

Hyde's grip loosened.

"How can a girl 'a your small stature and brain possibly hold the knowledge to suppress Covington?" Hyde shook his head, but his eyes were curious and wanted to hear what Ivy had to say.

"You will have to let me work. We have the materials here already. You will have to let me go, so I can show you. Please."

Hyde's grip loosened even more, "Do what ya must. Know that I will snap that twig of a neck'a yours, should you try anythin' funny lass."

She turned back to the hoodie she had filled with the research materials. Hyde's breath penetrated the hair hanging over the back of her neck. She held the heavy book in her right hand, and she used her left to move the artifacts as if she were looking for something with purpose.

"Stop fuckin' around," Hyde barked.

Ivy had one shot for his testicles. She would have to bend just a little for her elbow to smash his crotch. Her aim had to be true. She let an artifact drop off the table. With the motion to bend down to grab, she twisted and drove her right elbow into the lower regions of Mr. Hyde. He cowered, surprised at the sprite's strength.

"Ah! You bitch!"

"This bitch has two master's degrees you dick!" She held the textbook with both hands. All of her rage from losing her best friend channeled through her swing. The back of the book met Hyde's in violent, jerking, fashion. His head snapped back. Hyde was stunned, but not unconscious.

Ivy dropped the book and ran out of the lab. With her adrenaline pumping, she sprinted back towards the Institute.

Father Martinez drove the car as the invisible Andreij must have returned to his resting place at St. James. Bud was in the backseat and held the elixir safe with both hands.

"How is it that Maeve has suffered so many wounds my boy, especially the nasty one on her neck and back, and now barely lives with no heartbeat?" Father Martinez asked, keeping his eyes to the road.

"Maeve has the ability to set things on fire. She then absorbs the power of any supernatural creature she bests. We fought off zombies in Louisiana, therefore, she can sustain much damage and was even killed by a werewolf in Wales but lived. Or rather un-lived as it were. She also turns into a werewolf."

"Ah, monks like Maeve are especially rare. Her empathy towards every being causes the absorption. She is a true healer," Father Martinez said.

"Now it is our turn to heal her. Sadly, her human body can only take so much punishment. Upon observation of her undead status over the last few months, I noticed her strength wain. Being a zombie apparently does not give you sustained vitality. Eventually your body weakens. The zombie curse only animates the dead body for so long. So, I have spent the last few months trying to rid her of the curse and restart her heart to hopefully help her regain her live state."

"You will have your chance again soon. We are nearing the convent of Lourdes HS."

Bud looked at the elixir in his hands then out the window to a typical Southside neighborhood. Bungalows and Georgian style houses were all around. The corner of 55th and Pulaski had the typical trappings of this part of town, two gas stations, a donut shop, a bank, currency exchange and many Mexican restaurants. He felt comfort in this neighborhood and hoped Ivy was right, that the elixir would save Maeve.

Ivy reached the ladder. The same type of heavy footfalls that she had heard the night Tricia died echoed down the tunnel. She reached the floor of the dark Archaeological Institute. She pulled herself up next to the disturbed mummy burial. She would have to find a way through the broken display cases that blocked her exit. Ivy ran past the fallen relief and towards the lobby.

"Oh deary! I told ya I'd snap your twig of a' neck! Run all ya want I will catch up!" Hyde roared.

Ivy didn't let him intimidate her or slow her down. Her legs burned. Her heart pumped. Glass from the mummy's tornado crunched under her feet. Light from the lobby was showing through the hole Father Martinez had left earlier in the display case blockade. Ivy could feel her skin crawl as she felt Hyde get closer and closer.

"Love, you can't run or hide from Hyde! Hahaha!" His laugh was throaty, deep, and sinister.

Ivy dove through the path to the entryway and into the Institutes' lobby. Regular voices filled her ears, "Whoa there lady! What the hell is going on?" A security guard helped her up. He was surrounded by two policemen and a clean-up crew of maintenance men.

"Did you cause this mess?" The guard inquired.

Before Ivy could answer, Hyde broke through the display cases. One case almost crushed a janitor, who had opened the doors and had been preparing to clean up the mess.

Hyde emerged from the gallery. He looked bigger to Ivy.

A policeman yelled, "Don't move!" Hyde put his hands up.

"Dr. Covington?" One of the janitor's recognized Covington.

Hyde tore his tweed jacket off then pulled his shirt and tie in one fell swoop. His torso was hairy, muscular, and veiny.

"I said...don't move!" Both cops now had their side-arms drawn.

Hyde jumped at the policemen and tackled them. The guards and cleanup crew ran out of the Institute. Hyde grabbed the policemen's heads and bounced them off the hard floor. Blood pooled around them.

Hyde stood up and wiped the drool off his mouth, "You're next little Ivy."

Ivy ran as fast as she could out of the Institute and into Hyde Park, the neighborhood of Chicago Met University.

40

SAVE MAEVE

The convent was in the west wing of Lourdes High School. It had recently been rented by the Chicago Public Schools, to welcome neighborhood students of the Southside. Nuns no longer lived there and the school used the convent for storage. The yellow brick was typical of Catholic School construction in the early half of the twentieth century. The convent was abandoned until now.

Bud and Father Martinez entered through a back door.

"I couldn't bring her up any more floors. The second floor was the best I could do," Father Martinez said, holding his powerful cross.

"You said she would be safe here. How safe, Padre?" Bud coughed as the dust of the dark, creepy hallway attacked his throat. The hallway was long and there were small dorm rooms that populated each side.

Father Martinez pointed into a room to Bud's left.

"She protected her."

Bud followed the monk and looked into the room to see a floating nun wearing traditional garb. The habit was a white top surrounded by a black cape that framed her ghostly, old face. She rubbed Maeve's forehead in a comforting, peaceful fashion.

"This school is on all the haunted Chicago websites but she is actually here to protect the children not harm them."

Bud nodded his head. The nun's presence calmed him. He brought the elixir over to Maeve. Her eyes were open and Bud hoped she was glad to see him.

"Sister, could you help me raise her to a sitting position?" The nun smiled then disappeared.

"Sister Marguerite cannot touch the physical world. She was here to keep Maeve's soul with us, Bud."

Bud's eyes teared up. "Well, then thank God for her."

He lifted Maeve's head and torso up.

"Did I just hear you say thank God, Bud?" Father Martinez smiled.

"Not now. Christ! Can't you see we have to get her to ingest the elixir some way? The voice box I implanted should keep the liquid from seeping out of her jugular wound."

Maeve was able to open her mouth and Bud poured the elixir down her throat.

"Gentle my boy," Father Martinez said.

Bud slowed the pour. It took a while but he emptied Ivy's entire concoction into Maeve's stomach.

Bud and Father Martinez held her and stared, hoping something miraculous would happen.

"Perhaps we should lay her back down," Bud said.

Maeve's eyelids grew heavy.

"Maeve, my dear friend, stay with us. Perhaps we should summon Sister Marguerite."

Maeve's eyes closed.

"Father...summon Sister Marguerite!"

"Bud have faith. Give it some time my boy."

Bud was visibly upset. His shoulders raised and lowered quickly as he grabbed Maeve's hand. He cried hard.

"I am so sorry I couldn't help you, Maeve. So sorry!"

Tears rolled down his face in a flood that formed stains on his face.

Bud felt Maeve's hand grip his tightly. His posture straightened. He examined her.

Her color began to return to her face and hand. She pulled herself up to sitting position. The voice box fell out of the wound in her throat. Her vocal chords formed first, then the skin grew and bound her neck to its original pristine state.

She threw her head back as her spine cracked. The damage from her battles with the poltergeist healed.

She grew stronger and stronger before Bud's eyes.

The elixir worked. Ivy saved Maeve.

"Bud, thank you." Maeve's actual voice filled Bud's ears. She no longer sounded like a robot.

Bud tears continued as Maeve embraced and held him tight.

"You really should not thank me. There is someone you have to meet."

Maeve let go of him. Bud pulled out his phone and called Ivy.

She answered immediately, "Bud, did it... work?"

Bud noticed Ivy panting, "Are you running?" Bud asked.

"Yes, from Covington on campus! I am going to the Museum of Science and Industry! Meet me there! He killed Tricia! He is literally Jekyll and Hyde. Not kidding! Call the police!"

"Is that a good idea to lead him into a heavily populated museum?!" Bud asked.

Bud heard nothing. Ivy ended the call.

Bud dialed 9-1-1. "There is a murderer loose on the Chicago Metro campus chasing a petite woman of Chinese descent. You must hurry!"

He pushed the red end call icon.

"Bud, what is wrong with you? Did they even respond to you?" Maeve asked.

"Yes, of course. We must return to campus on the double quick!" Bud said.

Maeve shook her head.

41

SAVE IVY

"I can drive us back there," Father Martinez said, rushing into the hallway.

"We can get there faster. Bud can't you teleport us there?" Maeve asked.

"For some reason all the markers have been deactivated. I haven't any idea why. Can't we just fly with you?"

Maeve ran into the hallway to find a broom closet.

"Yes!" Maeve grabbed the broom and put it between her legs. Nothing happened. The broom didn't hover.

"Well, I am alive but seemed to have lost all my cool powers." Maeve dropped the broom.

"The car it is!" Bud said, following Father Martinez down the hall.

Ivy climbed the many steps of the green-domed, vast, Greco-Roman influence Museum of Science and Industry.

The school groups and main admissions desks were in the basement. She hoped to lead Hyde away from the crowds and school groups clamoring to get in. The Museum had already been open for an hour. Many people were already enjoying the popular exhibits like the human heart, whisper room, the hatchery, a U-boat, etc. She entered the building and pulled the nearest fire alarm.

The noise rattled her ears.

Families enjoying an intricate model train set, looked around to see if the alarm was legitimate. The Museum staff began to usher people to the nearest exits.

Ivy couldn't believe her cardiovascular health was as a good as it was. Sweat beaded on her forehead but she still pushed on. Hyde knocked people out of his way on the steps leading to the entrance. He entered the Museum, the exiting people scattered and screamed when he rushed in.

Ivy stopped to make sure he saw her.

She wanted his focus to still be on her and not the exiting crowds.

"There you are! My little Ivy!"

Ivy was a good hundred yards ahead of him. She ran to the interior of the Museum and took a sharp left and descended the stairs to the main floor to one of her favorite exhibits: the coal mine.

"There is a tree in Jackson Park just behind the Museum. The Order discovered a tree that needed protection there after the serial killer H.H. Holmes used the park to hunt for his victims. We can use it to contain the poltergeist should it attack again. If all of us say the prayer to St. Michael we should be able to defeat it." Father Martinez shared, while speeding eastward on 55th street back to Hyde Park.

"That poltergeist followed us home from Europe, Bud. That period of time we left the tree open for evil to escape, you know, between the werewolf battle and stopping Brother Mike? The poltergeist had to come out of the tree in Wales. It was haunting us and we didn't even know it until my wolf form could smell the damned thing," Maeve said.

"There was a considerable amount of time that the tree remained unsealed, while we dealt with Brother Mike. It is possible it escaped in that interim," Bud said.

"Why is it targeting us so viciously?" Maeve asked.

"In order for it to subsist in this realm and flourish, it needs to kill and haunt and spread evil. It needs to eliminate those that can stop it. Us." Father Martinez blew a red light, a camera behind the car flashed.

"You just got a ticket, Father."

"Bullshit, I never pay those anyway."

Maeve laughed.

"Could Covington and the poltergeist be connected? The elixir revived Maeve. Is it possible that it showed Covington clues to the elixir's existence to revive it?" Bud asked.

"The nature of poltergeists is to spread evil. Yes, they do form from the death of evil people. It revived evil remains with Capone and Mary but couldn't sustain the connection. The elixir could sustain the connection we can safely say," Maeve added.

"I wonder what evil person this poltergeist originates from?" Bud asked.

"Someone strong. Someone intimidating, who caused much death," Father Martinez added.

42

CANARY IN A COAL MINE

Ivy lowered herself onto the top of the open shaft elevator that brought guests down to the coal mine exhibit. The elevator was on the lower level which left a space between the top of the elevator and the ceiling of the mine. It was small enough for her to fit through. Ivy laid on her stomach and put her feet through the space first then scooted backwards. She dropped about five feet to the bituminous floor. She ran into the elevator and tried to pull the control panel open to prevent Hyde from using it and ultimately, take refuge in the coal mine.

She felt the elevator bounce.

"Ivy, this foolish game must cease. Are you down there? Did you fit your tiny twig body through this teeny space? Guess I should join you!"

The elevator bounced again. This time weight had been lifted from the top. Hyde was going for the call button.

Ivy pulled with all her might to bend the control panel to her will. It would not budge. There was no emergency stop in the elevator since it only traveled one floor.

The elevator power pulsed and it began to ascend slowly. Ivy kept pulling at the control panel trying to stop the elevator. She had few seconds to spare before she had to jump off the elevator to avoid Hyde.

"Come on! Come on!" Ivy pulled at the panel one last time. Her efforts proved futile. The elevator reached the main floor. Ivy was too late. Hyde stood over her.

"Hey there." His mouth stretched into a menacing, toothy grin.

The united monks of the Order sped down the Midway of Chicago Met's campus. The Museum of Science and Industry was in sight, as were many first responder vehicles with lights rotating. They were securing the perimeter and helping with the crowds pouring out on to the lawn.

"One can presume my call was effective!" Bud said.

"Not so fast, genius. This looks a fire alarm evacuation. You just called the cops! There are fire engines and trucks everywhere!" Maeve frowned, remembering how frustrating Bud could be.

Father Martinez drove as far as he could before a parked cop car blocked them. He pulled to the side of the road.

The three monks ran out of the car towards the south end of the Museum that borders Jackson Park.

Ivy cowered. Hyde grabbed her by the neck and lifted her up. Ivy clawed at his hands and arms.

"I take will great pleasure in crushin' ya throat little one!"

Suddenly, Hyde's eyes glowed a lightning blue color. He dropped Ivy to the floor. She watched as Hyde shook and the blue glow in his eyes permeated the rest of his body, similar to the reanimated mummy. The poltergeist possessed Hyde.

A group of firemen were clearing the area the coal mine was in.

"Hey big guy, can't you hear the alarm?! Let's go!"

Hyde stopped shaking. The poltergeist had gained full control. Hyde grabbed Ivy and put her over his shoulder.

"According to my master, you are useful to us. Your broken neck will have to wait."

There was a dining area behind the coal mine exhibit and a window that overlooked Jackson Park. Hyde ran and smashed through the window. Ivy screamed. Hyde stomped into a marsh in Jackson Park.

43

THE ORDER POWER

Bud, Maeve, and Father Martinez heard a scream and saw Hyde, glowing blue bound into Jackson Park's marsh with Ivy on his shoulder. His progress was slow in the muddy water.

"He has Ivy and appears to be enhanced by the poltergeist!" Bud yelled.

"We can kill two birds with one stone! Like I said, there is a tree we can seal the poltergeist in within the Park's grounds!" Father Martinez said.

The three monks of the Order ran to cut off Hyde.

"There it is! By that small bridge where the marsh narrows is the tree we can seal the poltergeist in!" Father Martinez yelled.

"Maeve is it possible for you to still set things ablaze?" Bud ran ahead of his two companions.

"Yes, that I learned from my Uncle with my training. I didn't absorb it from any ghouls," Maeve answered.

"Can you set ablaze the perimeter of the marsh he is in?" Bud asked.

"Yes, I believe I can." Maeve held her cross in stride and said a prayer.

The grass around the marsh burst into flame. Hyde reached the bridge. The fire started to lick at the bridge and Hyde had nowhere to go but forward and towards the tree.

The three monks were now close, just outside the marsh. The flames grew higher. The bridge succumbed to the inferno.

Hyde lifted Ivy over his head with both arms as if to body slam her.

"I will kill her you fools!" Hyde barked.

The haze caused from the flames distorted the scene and Hyde and Ivy appeared to bend.

"Father, is it possible for you to throw a light shield around Ivy as you brilliantly executed earlier?" Bud asked.

Without hesitation, "Espiritu Santo!" A beam of light shot from Father Martinez's cross and showered Ivy in beautiful sparkles.

"Perhaps now would be a good time to pray."

"Has your faith been restored, Bud?" Father Martinez asked.

"I believe so, Father. I believe so." Bud looked at Maeve.

The three monks of the Order recited the prayer:

"St. Michael the Archangel, defend us in
battle. Be our defense against the wicked-
ness and snares of the devil. May God re-
buke him, we humbly pray, and do thou,
O Prince of the heavenly hosts, thrust
into hell Satan, and all the evil spirits, who
prowl the about the world seeking the ruin
of souls. Amen."

Hyde dropped Ivy into the marsh. He keeled over. The
poltergeist within him began to separate from his body.
The blue ghostly form was being pulled into the tree. It
tried to repossess Hyde but failed. The power of three
monks of the Order of St. Michael proved too great. The
tree behind absorbed the poltergeist, banishing it back into
the realm from whence it came.

The flames around the marsh died down. Bud and
Maeve jumped in to Ivy's aid. She still glowed from the
light shield.

Bud and Maeve helped her out of the muddy water.
Hyde had transformed back into Covington. He lay unconscious on his back, slowly sinking in to the marsh. Bud
dragged him out.

The threat had been contained. The Order was
victorious.

44

RESOLUTE AND
IRRESOLUTE

"The police have officially arrested your husband for the murder of Tricia Pazinski. One thing I have to ask is what pizza place did you go to the night of her murder and at what time Mrs. Covington?"

Her raspy voice responded through Bud's phone, "We went to D'Ags at about 8:30 after he was done working in his office upstairs. How could it have been him? He was home I swear."

"I am afraid your husband had been experimenting with a poisonous substance that caused dissociative identity disorder. He literally had a split personality. He murdered Tricia then escaped the Institute through a hidden tunnel that exited onto a soccer field on the

University's campus. Upon his escape, he must have switched back to his normal self to join you for pizza as if he'd never left."

"But... why would he kill that girl? I thought he loved her?" Mrs. Covington kept her composure, even though that last sentence had to hurt.

"Your husband was drinking a substance that contained mercury. It overstimulated his amygdala, the part of the brain where aggression forms. The chemist on my team believes he killed her while identifying as his more violent dangerous personality. She was helping him with his research. He was trying to get the Board of Regent's position, as I am sure you know. Perhaps stress caused him to turn on her or maybe she was trying to get him to stop experimenting on himself with this phony ancient elixir," Bud explained.

"Well, thank you for your help Hutchins. I truly appreciate it."

"I am sure you will see your husband on television tonight. He caused quite a stir on campus and nearly killed two police officers. Goodbye, ma'am." Bud ended the call.

"That was a bit of a harsh way to end the call Bud!" Maeve said.

"What?" Bud shrugged.

Father Martinez stopped the car in front of Bud's grandfather's home. Maeve, Ivy and Bud exited.

"May God bless and keep you all. I am back to St. James. It was quite an adventure Mr. Hutchins." Father Martinez stuck his head out the car window.

"Indeed it was, Father. Thank you for all your blessed assistance."

Father kissed his cross then drove off.

"Did you ever figure out why your teleport tech failed, Bud?" Ivy asked matching their pace to the front door.

"No, I hope to get Bert back up and running to see what occurred. I have a query for you, Ivy. Why didn't Hyde kill you?"

"I think the poltergeist knew I developed the elixir correctly. Hyde would have killed me but that is when the poltergeist possessed him. He told me I was useful to them." Ivy used air quotes.

"Perhaps." Bud turned the keys in the lock and entered the house. He felt comfort to see his grandparent's home.

"Um, Bud?" Maeve pointed to all the picture frames that were broken and thrown on the floor. Bud's grandfather had been torn from every picture.

Bud picked up the picture of him and his Grandfather downtown at Christmas. His Grandfather's face had been burned from it. Maeve patted his back in comfort.

Bud ran to Bert's computer room. The room had been ransacked and destroyed.

"This is why the teleportation stopped working. They destroyed my computer. That is what maintained the network communication between the band and destination markers." Bud frantically searched his desk. He threw the keyboard. Bert's head was gone.

Underneath the keyboard, burned into the wood was the tree symbol Hanks had showed him a few months ago. It was from the cult that Brother Mike was associated with. This was the cult that had destroyed Bud's home, stole Bert's data, and murdered monks of the Order of St. Michael.

Maeve, Ivy, and Bud Hutchins stared at each other. Their victorious moods had been soured by yet another relentless evil.

END

The ELIXIR: A BUD HUTCHINS URBAN FANTASY

Visit MisterMichaels.com, the official site of Author JB Michaels for TWO FREE BOOKS!

The Works of JB

With over 500 pages of action adventure and thrills, these individual books have earned a recommended Kirkus review, 3 awards, 11 five star badges from Readers' Favorite and over 50 positive reviews on Amazon.

The Order of St. Michael: A Bud Hutchins Thriller

The Tannenbaum Tailors and the Secret Snowball *(Gold Medal- Readers' Favorite International Book Awards 2017) (National Indie Excellence Award Finalist)*

The Tannenbaum Tailors and the Brethren of the Saints *(Kirkus Reviews Recommended Book) (Bronze Medal- Readers' Favorite International Book Awards 2017)*

Made in the USA
Middletown, DE
29 March 2019